Red, meet the Wolf

"Sorry to do this, but I'm sitting there," he drawled, pointing to the seat next to me, "so I think I'm gonna have to trouble you to get up for a sec."

That voice. I could have listened to it for at least three lifetimes. It was just so . . . *twangy*.

As we did the airplane aisle dance so he could get in, we bumped arms and an electric shock shot down my spine. Omigod—I knew it. We were soul mates!

Once he was settled in his seat, he turned to me. "I like your hat," he said, pointing at the red cowboy hat I had bought the day before.

"Thanks," I replied.

He shook his head and laughed.

"What?" I asked.

"I was just thinking," he drawled. "You're probably trouble with a capital *T*. Red cowboy hat kinda girls always are." As he winked at me, another jolt of electricity went through me. But this time it went *up* instead of down. "But that's okay—'cause sometimes trouble can be fun." Even though our seats were supposed to stay in their upright positions, he put his back. "Must be fate that I ended up getting this Michael guy's seat, huh?" he said with a wolfish smile.

He had no idea.

OTHER BOOKS YOU MAY ENJOY

An Abundance of Katherines	John Green
A Non-Blonde Cheerleader in Love	Kieran Scott
Brunettes Strike Back	Kieran Scott
Cindy Ella	Robin Palmer
A Countess Below Stairs	Eva Ibbotson
Enthusiasm	Polly Shulman
Geek Charming	Robin Palmer
I Was a Non-Blonde Cheerleader	Kieran Scott
Just Listen	Sarah Dessen
Let it Snow	John Green, Maureen Johnson, and Lauren Myracle

Little Miss Red

ROBIN PALMER

speak

An Imprint of Penguin Group (USA) Inc.

SPEAK

Published by the Penguin Group

Penguin Group (USA) Inc., 345 Hudson Street, New York, New York 10014, U.S.A.

Penguin Group (Canada), 90 Eglinton Avenue East, Suite 700,
Toronto, Ontario, Canada M4P 2Y3 (a division of Pearson Penguin Canada Inc.)

Penguin Books Ltd, 80 Strand, London WC2R 0RL, England

Penguin Group Ireland, 25 St Stephen's Green, Dublin 2, Ireland
(a division of Penguin Books Ltd)

Penguin Group (Australia), 250 Camberwell Road, Camberwell, Victoria 3124, Australia
(a division of Pearson Australia Group Pty. Ltd)

Penguin Books India Pvt. Ltd., 11 Community Centre,
Panchsheel Park, New Delhi - 110 017, India

Penguin Group (NZ), 67 Apollo Drive, Rosedale, North Shore 0632, New Zealand
(a division of Pearson New Zealand Ltd)

Penguin Books (South Africa) (Pty) Ltd, 24 Sturdee Avenue,
Rosebank, Johannesburg 2196, South Africa

Registered Offices: Penguin Books Ltd, 80 Strand, London WC2R 0RL, England

Published by Speak, an imprint of Penguin Group (USA) Inc., 2009

1 3 5 7 9 10 8 6 4 2

Copyright © Robin Palmer, 2010

LIBRARY OF CONGRESS CATALOGING-IN-PUBLICATION DATA IS AVAILABLE UPON REQUEST

Speak ISBN 978-0-14-241123-0

Printed in the United States of America

For Laila Nabulsi,

for patiently listening to *my* drama

over the years

Acknowledgments

Immense gratitude to Penguin's Jennifer Bonnell and Kristin Gilson, for their brilliant editorial guidance; Eileen Kreit, for her unwavering support; and Kristin Smith, for her amazing eye.

Kate Lee, for taking care of everything.

Amy Loubalu and Christina Beck, for living it with me.

And for Ken Palmer, the best dad in the world, for looking at me across the table at Carousel that night and telling me not to give up.

Little Miss Red

prologue

I'm very big on signs. So when the captain announced that our flight to Florida would be delayed because of some last-minute passengers, I took that as yet another sign that this trip was going to be a disaster. With all the drama that had been going on the last few days, it was obvious that I needed to get out of Los Angeles, but spending my Spring Break with my grandmother at a retirement community was a little too *un*dramatic.

I turned my iPhone back on, sure I was going to find a text from my semi-ex-boyfriend, Michael, saying he had changed his mind and wanted to get back together, but like the other ten times I had checked that morning, there was nothing.

After making sure it was off again (the captain hadn't given the "Please make sure all electronic devices are off" announcement, but I certainly didn't want to forget and be responsible for a plane crash), I took out *Propelled* by *Passion*, the latest book in the Devon Devoreaux romance series. As I gazed at Dante, the tank top-wearing, motorcycle-riding complete and utter hottie on the cover, I felt my muscles relax. Something about his blue eyes and the ridges of his ripped abs always calmed me down. I knew many of my fellow juniors at Castle Heights High had written English papers about how Heathcliff from *Wuthering Heights* was the most romantic hero in literary history, but as far as I was concerned, he had *nothing* on Dante.

As riveting and dramatic as the story was, before I knew it, my eyelids felt like they were being yanked down by elves, thanks to the Benadryl I had taken. Soon enough, everything fell away, even my seatmate Harriet's nonstop chatter and the meowing of her cat, which was stowed in her carry-on and giving me an allergy attack. I was just about to doze off when fate intervened, my life did a complete one-eighty, and was changed forever.

"Excuse me, but I need to get by," I heard a gravelly voice with a slight twang say.

As my eyes fluttered open, I thought that the Benadryl must have *really* kicked in, because that was the only thing that could explain the hallucination I was having.

"Dante!" I gasped.

The guy standing in front of me looked confused. "Who's Dante?"

I looked back down at my book. Okay, the guy standing

in front of me was more like nineteen rather than in his early thirties, and his hair was more the color of dark chocolate than Dante's roasted chestnut mop, and sure, his eyes were the color of caramel rather than sky blue, and he was wearing a faded black T-shirt rather than a formfitting, ab-rocking white tank top, but still—the resemblance was *crazy*. They could have been brothers.

I quickly turned the book over. "Uh . . . no one," I replied.

"Sorry to do this, but I'm sitting there," he drawled, pointing to the seat next to me, "so I think I'm gonna have to trouble you to get up for a sec."

That voice. I could have listened to it for at least three lifetimes. It was just so . . . *twangy*.

"You're 12B?" I said, confused.

After reaching into the pocket of his jeans and looking at his boarding pass, he nodded. "But . . . Michael was 12B."

He looked confused again. The way he furrowed his brow was beyond sexy. "Who's Michael?"

"Michael . . . is . . ." What to say? "Not here," I finally finished.

As we did the airplane aisle dance so he could get in, we bumped arms and an electric shock shot down my spine. Omigod—I knew it. We were soul mates! The exact same thing happened when Devon met Dante the first time.

Once he was settled in his seat, he turned to me. "I

like your hat," he said, pointing at the red cowboy hat I had bought the day before.

"Thanks," I replied.

He shook his head and laughed.

"What?" I asked.

"I was just thinking," he drawled. "You're probably trouble with a capital *T*. Red cowboy hat kinda girls always are." As he winked at me, another jolt of electricity went through me. But this time it went *up* instead of down. "But that's okay—'cause sometimes trouble can be fun." Even though our seats were supposed to stay in their upright positions, he put his back. "Must be fate that I ended up getting this Michael guy's seat, huh?" he said with a wolfish smile.

He had no idea.

one

Some people—actually, a lot of people, if you go by the amount of bumper stickers on the road—lead their lives according to the slogan "WWJD?" *What would Jesus do?*

But because I, Sophie Rebecca Greene, of Studio City, California, am an Aquarian and therefore tend to break away from the pack, my motto ever since I was thirteen has been "WWDDD?"

What would Devon Devoreaux do?

"Okay, you guys," I said to my two best friends, Jordan and Ali, that April afternoon in the cafeteria as I took a bite of my smoked turkey and Swiss sandwich. "This is serious—WWDDD?"

Jordan rolled her eyes. "She wouldn't do anything, because she doesn't actually *exist*. She's a made-up character." Jordan's mom was Lulu Lavoie, the award-winning writer and creator of the Devon Devoreaux series, so she loved to point this out.

I sighed. I loved my friends, but life can sometimes be very lonely when you're as creative and passionate as I am and your friends just . . . aren't. "Well, if she *did* exist, and she were in a calendar, what month would she be?" I asked.

The week before, during our bimonthly meeting of the French club, I had come up with the brilliant idea that we do a Castle Heights calendar to raise money for next year's trip to Montreal. Everyone loved the idea, but I had to admit my motives were a little more selfish than just wanting to stay in a hotel and order room service. I had gotten the idea from Devon, actually. Back when she was sixteen and still living in Wasilla, Alaska, Devon had been Miss February in a "Find a Cure for Epilepsy" calendar, and a big modeling agent happened to see it. Within months she was on the cover of *Cosmopolitan* and leading a jet-set life. It wasn't that I wanted to become a model (there weren't a lot of auburn-haired, freckled girls on the cover of *Teen Vogue*), but I was hoping that the calendar would jump-start my life—take me out of an existence of boring, extracurricular clubs and SAT prep classes and lead me to the adventure-filled life that I knew was my destiny.

When my iPhone buzzed, I lunged for it. According to some people (okay, everyone who knew me), I was a little . . . *addicted* to it. Yes, it was true that I had had a slight panic attack when I got to school one morning and realized I had left it at home, but you never knew when an e-mail was going to come through that could just possibly change your life forever.

As I looked at the screen, I realized that, unfortunately, this one wasn't one of those. It was just an update from the Lulu Lavoie Fan Club announcing that her new book was now available for preorder on Amazon.

"Anyway, I was thinking April would be a good month," I continued. "Not only is it hopeful, but it would get a lot of traffic because people would turn to it to count how many weeks till Spring Break."

After adjusting her bandana, Jordan jammed half a Ho Ho into her mouth. "I can't believe I'm being an accessory to my best friend willingly objectifying her body to be a pinup girl. If any members of the Young Feminists of the New Millennium club find out, they'll impeach me," she said. Jordan had recently been sworn in as president after Marla Warner announced she was resigning to try out for cheerleading.

I shrugged. "If it were July or August and I was wearing a bathing suit, I could see how it would be cheesy, but I'm thinking of a sundress and a little cardigan. You know . . . cute sexy."

"Cute sexy instead of Juliet DeStefano sexy sexy?" Ali asked as she bit into her Weight Watchers caramel cake. Ali didn't need to diet—she just loved the aftertaste of the Weight Watchers stuff.

Jordan kicked her under the table. "Um, hello?

7

Remember the no-Juliet-DeStefano-talk-ever rule that we passed last week?" she whispered.

If I couldn't have Devon's life (at least not until I graduated from college and moved to New York City or Paris or London), I would have settled for Juliet's. Jordan was always saying I was completely obsessed with her, but that wasn't true. I was only *mildly* obsessed with her. I mean, how could a person *not* be? From the very first day she arrived as a transfer student back in December—when I, as a member of the Castle Heights Greeters, was assigned to give her a tour of the school—I just *knew* the story that she had moved here from Wichita, Kansas, because her dad was transferred was just a cover for something else. Okay, maybe it was just an honest mistake when Mrs. Winkler, the school secretary, kept calling her Julia instead of Juliet in the office that morning—but maybe not. Maybe Juliet had changed her name from Julia because she was on the run like Devon in *Fueled by Fear*, when Devon's affair with the Olympic swimmer ended and he started stalking her. And what about when, in making small talk during the tour, she revealed that she had moved six times since third grade? She said her father was a college professor and that's why she kept switching schools, but there was something about the story I found a little fishy.

Also, she only ever spoke to Phan, a Cambodian exchange student. Ali thought that this was either because Juliet was shy or because all the other girls were completely jealous that she was a super hottie, but I didn't buy it. I thought she was afraid that if she made friends for whom English was their first language, she'd have to weave a web of lies to cover up her past and wouldn't be able to keep them straight, ultimately having a nervous breakdown like Devon in *Crazy with Control*. Regardless, Jordan and Ali were right; she was definitely sexy sexy. With the body and face of a Victoria's Secret model and the way she could take her long, silky brown hair and, with the flick of her wrist, twist it into a messy-yet-sexy bun, every boy in school was in love with her. Whether the rumors about her and the football team were true, no one knew, but it *was* true that they stopped dead in their tracks and their jaws fell to the floor when she walked down the hall. Like Devon, she had the ability to turn men into "quivering masses of desire." I mean, who *wouldn't* want to be Juliet DeStefano?

I put down my sandwich. "Maybe I *want* to be objectified," I announced.

Jordan gave me the same kind of horrified look as when I ordered a hamburger during her Vegans Unite phase.

One of my Grandma Roz's favorite sayings was, "The grass may be greener on the other side, but you still have to mow the lawn." Maybe, but a lot of the time I felt like my patch of lawn was dry and brown and dead, whereas people like Devon and Juliet had green and dewy lawns filled with exotic flowers like birds-of-paradise.

"Okay, maybe 'objectified' isn't the right word," I continued. "What I want is to be *seen*."

"We see you," Ali offered. "Especially now that the eye doctor changed my prescription." She pushed her new glasses up the bridge of her nose.

"Yeah, but no one else does. I just . . . blend in." I motioned to the cafeteria. "Look at us—we're not popular," I said, pointing to the Ramp where all the A-listers sat. "And we're not *un*popular," I said, pointing to the video game geeks, goths, and stoners sitting around the periphery. I sighed. "We sit smack in the middle. We just . . . *are*."

"But what if 'just being' is the whole point of life!" said Ali, whose mom was a Buddhist.

"Yeah, well, I don't want to just *be*—I want to *do*! I want to *live*! I want to *stand out*!"

Jordan pointed to the magenta streak in her blonde hair that was peeking out from underneath the bandana she started wearing when she became a Young Feminist.

"I still have some dye left if you want to color your hair," she offered.

"No thanks," I sighed. That wasn't the kind of living I was looking for. I wanted something bigger. More, I don't know, *dramatic*.

WWDDD? I thought. I wasn't entirely sure, but I had an idea of where she might start: break up with Michael Rosenberg, my boyfriend of three years who I loved, but was no longer *in* love with.

"No offense, Sophie," Jordan said after school as we were getting manicures at Kathy's Nails on Ventura Boulevard, near where we both lived. "But Michael's the only boyfriend you've ever had. So how do you know you're not *in* love with him?"

"You just know," I replied. "It's like in your mom's book *Seduced by Seduction*, when Devon meets the Saudi Arabian sheik at the Cannes Film Festival and he gives her a 22-carat diamond engagement ring the next day. That's *in* love."

"But Michael's great," Jordan said. "I mean, what other guy are you going to find who likes going to the mall and isn't gay?"

She did have a point.

"And Jeremy would be beyond bummed if you guys broke up," she added.

Jeremy was my nine-year-old brother. He loved Michael, and would even hug him, which for someone with Asperger's syndrome said a lot.

I flinched as Kathy pushed down the cuticles on my short nails. "I just don't know if that's enough anymore, though," I said. "I want *passion*. Not someone to go shopping with or play Go Fish with me and my little brother."

"What color you want?" asked Kathy when she was done massaging my hands with hand cream.

I pointed at the bottle of Dark as Midnight that I had

picked out. Dark as Midnight was so . . . dark. And sultry. And sophisticated. Devon kept a bottle of it in every one of her designer handbags.

Kathy shook her head like she had water in her ears. "I tell you every time—make your stubby fingers look even shorter!" she brayed.

"But—" My iPhone buzzed.

"Watch out!" Kathy barked as I knocked over a bottle of remover while grabbing for the phone.

"Sorry," I replied, clicking into the text. **Yo what up? Can't come for dinner—SAT prep class. M.** it said. Although he was a white boy from Encino, Michael was very into rap. Which is why every conversation with him had lots of "Yo's" and "Check it's." I sighed. I had been hoping that maybe if we spent more quality time together it would reignite our passion, but apparently that wasn't going to happen tonight.

"Plus, the dark colors look horrible when they chip," Jordan added. Her nails were being painted clear, which was the only color the Young Feminists were allowed to wear. "My mom has to get hers done like every other day for that very reason."

Kathy picked up a bottle of boring pale pink. "We do Cotton Candy, like always," she announced. "You just not Dark as Midnight kind of girl!"

I had learned long ago it was useless to try and fight with Kathy about nail color. Rumor had it that pre-*Friends*, she was always talking Jennifer Aniston out of Dark as Midnight as well.

"Fine," I agreed half-heartedly. But as soon as I moved to the side of the lawn with the birds-of-paradise it was going to be Dark as Midnight on my fingers *and* toes.

"I think you should wait until after Mexico to make your decision about Michael," said Jordan.

"Good idea," I agreed. I was going to Puerto Vallarta for Spring Break with Jordan and her mom to spend the week at the cliffside villa Lulu had bought after selling the movie rights to her second book, *Ravished by Regret*, the one where Devon falls in love with the Italian count who was also a billionaire dot-com guy who had come up with an Italian knockoff of Facebook. It would be the perfect place to search my soul and decide whether the fact that I'd rather do my trig homework rather than make out with my boyfriend was a passing thing, or if we really weren't meant to be.

Unfortunately, as Grandma Roz also liked to say, "You make your plans and God laughs."

Like when the person who owns the vacation house cancels the trip after finding out she has to do a major rewrite of her latest book because her editor has accused her of plagiarizing herself.

"So Daddy and I have a surprise for you," cooed Mom at dinner a few nights later, as she plunked a piece of liver down on my plate that night. (A typical conversation with

13

my mother: Mom: It's for your anemia. Me: But I'm not anemic. Mom: *Exactly*—because you eat your liver!)

Mom only cooed like this when she was trying to get Jeremy to turn off the TV or when she was about to tell me something I wasn't going to like.

"What is it?" I said warily, shading my eyes from the glare that was coming off the freshly painted yellow walls of our kitchen. Mom had recently redecorated our entire house to make it more "serenity-friendly." Because it was like every other Spanish-style house in Studio City, wood and darker colors worked best, but that hadn't stopped her from choosing so-called happy colors like yellow, lavender, and peach. I felt like I was living in a tub of rainbow sherbet. When I grew up, I was going to paint my entire New York City penthouse apartment red, just like Devon did. All the magazines said that red was the most passionate color.

After plunking down a piece of liver on Jeremy's plate (which he immediately pushed away before going back to making ruler-straight rows of peas), she sat down and took my hand in her own Cotton Candy–painted one. Even though I had seen the video of Mom holding me in the hospital right after I was born, I still sometimes wondered if it had been a switched-at-birth situation. My parents were great, but as an accountant (Dad) and a shrink (Mom) they were both so . . . normal. I knew at my very core that I was supposed to have a page-turner kind of life, so wouldn't it make more sense for me to come from a family full of CIA agents or something?

"I talked to Grandma Roz this morning," Mom started to say, pushing her auburn hair off her face. (Mine was the same shade, so I guess there was no denying we were related.)

The back of my neck started to itch. Just hearing Grandma Roz's name made me nervous. Unlike other grandmothers who were sweet and cuddly and who did things like tell you how brilliant you are and sneak you five-dollar bills, Grandma Roz was like the poster person for cranky old people.

"Did she call with a new burial outfit update?" I asked. At seventy-five, Grandma Roz was still in perfect health, but that hadn't stopped her from spending every day for the last fifteen years talking about who was going to get what when she died.

Mom let go of my hand and reached over to Jeremy to try and get him to eat some of his liver, but he was having none of it, which made sense for a kid with an IQ of 165. Unlike me and Mom, Jeremy took after my dad—darker hair and a big nose.

"No. She called to say she wants the silver candelabras back," Mom said.

The candelabras were the only thing of value that my great-great-grandparents had been able to take with them when they left Poland. Legend had it that getting them to

America involved a train, a ship, and a mule. They had been passed down from generation to generation as a wedding gift and now lived in our dining room, where Jeremy liked to compulsively polish them (which, Dad said, was one of the few pluses of Asperger's).

"Why does she want them back?" I asked.

"She says that because she has so little in her life that makes her happy, having them around as she gets ready to die might make her feel better."

Dad looked up from his liver, which, he too wasn't eating. "And you wonder why I'm a glass-half-empty type of person," he grumbled to Mom.

She turned to him. "Larry, please don't take out your resentment toward your mother in front of the kids. You know how children mirror what they see, and I don't want them to be talking about us like this down the road." She turned back to me and took my hand again. "Anyway, I told Grandma I'd ship them to her—I told her I'd even send them FedEx, even though they're so heavy it would cost me more than your Bat Mitzvah did—but she says that the worry during transit time would kill her. So when I mentioned that your Spring Break plans had gotten cancelled—"

I pulled my now-clammy hand out of hers. "You're going to make me spend Spring Break in the Garden of Eden?!" I squawked. It may have sounded fancy, but the Garden of Eden—located in hot and humid Delray

Beach—was probably the least luxurious retirement community in all of Florida. Unfortunately, even though Grandma Roz was superrich because her father was the founder of TeePeeMatic, the company that invented the little tube that holds toilet paper rolls in the holder, she worried about money all the time.

Mom nodded and gave me The Smile, the one where the corners of her mouth reached up so high they almost hit her eyes. It was the smile she used when she was trying to talk me into something I *really* didn't want to do. Like visiting my grandmother. "Aren't you excited?" she cooed. "You're going to have so much fun!"

I could tell from the way she squeezed my hand to the point where I started to lose feeling that there would be no discussion. Instead of hanging out at home and going to the movies during my vacation, I'd be surrounded by bottles of aspirin and Tums.

"But that's not the best part," Mom said.

"*Best* part?!" I cried. "I'm still waiting for the *good* part!"

"I talked to Marci today"—Marci was Michael's mom— "and she's decided to send Michael to visit *his* grandmother too, so you'll be able to spend Spring Break *together*! With lots of sunscreen, obviously."

Michael's grandmother Rose lived one town over from Delray Beach, in Boca Raton, in the superdeluxe Fountain of Youth Senior Living Village. Not only were there two pools instead of one, but there were four water aerobics and Yoga for Seniors classes a day.

"Isn't that *great*?!" Mom asked.

I know I was lucky that my parents trusted Michael and me so much, but that was part of the problem. We could have been in my bedroom with the door locked—not that we did that—and they would know that all we were doing was watching TV. So much for having some time apart to figure things out. "Yeah. I can't wait," I mumbled, dragging my fork over my peas and making a mess before glancing over at Jeremy, who looked like he was going to cry. Disorganization freaked him out. "Sorry," I said, patting him on the arm. "I'll stop."

Mom turned to my dad. "Larry, you know that Dr. Heath said that it's very important that we present a united front to the kids," she hissed. Dr. Heath was their couples therapist. "So help me out here, please."

"Okay, okay." He cleared his throat and turned to me. "Honey, you make it sound like we're sending you to one of those wilderness camps," he said. "It's Florida. People love Florida."

"Yeah, old people and serial killers," I mumbled. I glanced at my iPhone, praying it would buzz with an e-mail from Jordan saying the trip to Mexico was miraculously back on.

"*And*—you'll love this," Mom said, ignoring me. "Marci was even able to get you seats next to each other on the same flight!"

18

Obviously, I had no say in the matter, as the tickets were already booked. "That's great," I replied. I sounded about as excited as Jeremy when he was told he had to go to school. Basically, my Spring Break would be the same as my weekends: watching television with the boyfriend I was not *in* love with. The only difference was that instead of Michael's giant plasma screen and the good snacks, we'd be sitting on my grandmother's plastic-covered couch eating Coffee Nips.

"I have a feeling this just might be your best Spring Break *ever*," Mom said. "Now help me clear the table."

"Yo, what up?" Michael said later that night when he called. I was in my newly painted, lavender-colored bedroom supposedly working on a paper for English class about Zelda Fitzgerald, the wife of F. Scott Fitzgerald (the author of *The Great Gatsby*) who ultimately went crazy and ended up in a mental hospital (most likely because she loved him so much). But really what I was doing was watching a special I had TiVo'd on SOAPnet called *The Top 100 Greatest Love Affairs in Soap History*. People were always talking about how romantic Angelina Jolie and Brad Pitt were, but they had *nothing* on Luke and Laura, this couple from *General Hospital* who fell madly in love in the eighties and managed to stay together through all sorts of crazy things like kidnappings and faked deaths.

"Hey," I replied from my bed with its serenity-friendly

yellow/pink/peach comforter as I saved my work on my laptop.

"So, what up?" he asked, the TV blaring in the background.

I looked at my watch. Yup. He was watching *MTV Cribs*. Just like he did every weeknight. I got off my bed and walked over to turn off the tinkling feng shui–approved, serenity-boosting fountain on my desk. I don't know if it made me happy, but it *did* make me feel like I had to pee all the time. "Not much. So I guess we're going to Florida together for Spring Break," I said, trying to sound excited.

It hadn't always been like this—there *was* a time I was madly in love with him. In fact, the minute I set eyes on him at Faryl Reingold's Bat Mitzvah in seventh grade, I knew we were meant to be together, just like Devon felt when she saw that sexy painter from Oklahoma standing at the top step of his Chelsea loft in *Doused by Desire*. After that day, we were inseparable. While all the boys I knew were into video games, Michael was different. Not only did my parents approve—because they knew his parents from temple and liked them very much— but Michael liked to talk for hours and watch TV rather than play sports. And because he was an only child and his mother was a shopaholic, he had spent his child- hood sitting outside dressing rooms. So not only was he super-patient, but he could spot an amazing deal from fifty yards away.

There was no answer other than the TV.

"Michael?" I asked.

Still no answer. Nowadays he did this all the time. *He* called *me*, but then he spent the entire call watching TV and not paying attention. The days where we'd talk for hours about nothing and everything were long gone.

"Michael!" I shouted.

"Huh?"

"I said, I guess we're going to Florida together."

"Oh. Yeah. That'll be cool, huh?"

"Uh huh," I agreed, plopping back down on my bed. I picked up my dog-eared copy of *Lassoed by Lust* that I kept on my nightstand and traced my finger across Dante Jackson's jaw on the cover. All of the guys on the covers of Lulu's novels were hotties, but Dante was the hottest of them all. With his perfectly faded Levis, and his tight white tank clinging to his ripped pecs, and his fingernails with just the *teensiest* bit of dirt underneath them (because he was a rancher and therefore a very hard worker), Dante was exactly my kind of guy. I *love* ranchers. Granted, because I'm allergic to horses I've never been anywhere near a ranch and therefore the only ones I've seen have been on television or in movies, but they seem to be a freakishly attractive group of people.

"So, what else is going on?" I asked him.

"Huh? Oh, nothing." He was *so* not paying attention to our conversation. I bet when guys called Juliet DeStefano, they paid attention to *her*. And I *knew* they paid attention to Devon, because in *Bowled Over by Bliss*, the Indian customer service representative racked up a thousand-dollar cell phone bill one month after falling in love with the sound of her voice when she called with a question about her computer.

"Then why'd you call?" I asked.

"Because I always call you at nine," he replied. That was true. The good news with Michael was that there were no surprises. The bad news with Michael was that there were no surprises. If he said he'd call at nine, he called at nine. If he said we were going for pizza, we'd go for pizza. Mom says I should consider myself beyond lucky to have a boyfriend who "provides me with consistency"—that hopefully getting into that habit so early in my life will make it so that when I grow up I don't end up choosing men who are "emotionally unavailable" like most of her patients seem to do. But ever since junior year started, it was as if that . . . *thing*—the thing that Devon called *je ne sais quoi,* which is French for "I do not know what"—has been gone from our relationship.

"But I'm gonna go now because this is one of my favorite *MTV Cribs* episodes. I'll call you tomorrow at nine."

"Okay," I sighed. That was the problem—not just with Michael, but with everything in my life. It was all just so . . . *scheduled*. Between French club and yearbook staff and SAT prep classes and piano lessons there was no room for what Devon called "happy accidents," a.k.a. fate, to intervene. Just *once* I would have liked to mix it up and do something out of the ordinary.

I picked up *Lassoed by Lust.* "I bet you don't even *own* a watch," I said to Dante.

two

Because it was Spring Break season, there was a massive amount of pre-tanning going on in L.A. Over the last few weeks, the brightness level in the city had been dropping every day.

"That girl looks like a leather chair," said Jordan as we sat in the Farmer's Market the next afternoon waiting for Michael before going over to the Dell, a mall. I had originally been planning to get some stuff for Puerto Vallarta, but now that I would be stuck with Grandma Roz, I figured I'd focus on finding the perfect outfit to wear for the calendar photo shoot. The winners wouldn't be announced until the day before Spring Break, but because I had voted for myself fifty-four times using made-up e-mail addresses (obviously, it if was against the rules I never would have done it, but there was nothing in there about multiple voting), I was pretty sure Miss April was mine.

The Farmer's Market was a collection of tons of

different restaurants and food stands that had been there forever, as had most of the people who walked around there. Even though you could get everything from tacos to Korean food to cookies, I always went for the same thing: an apple cider donut from Bob's Donuts. The one day I tried to shake things up and asked for a Boston cream, Al, the guy behind the counter, just shook his head and said, "Nah, you're not a Boston cream kinda girl, kid. Too messy for you."

"Look—there's Dylan Schoenfield," Ali said, pointing to a girl with long, blond hair who was a senior at Castle Heights. She was leaving Du-par's restaurant with Josh Rosen, another senior. Her dad owned the Dell. "I'd do anything for my hair to be as blond and straight as hers," Ali sighed, as she ran her hand through her own dark, frizzy curls.

"I heard it's because she gets that Japanese straightening thing done to it," Jordan said. "That's what my mom does," she went on. "It costs almost a thousand dollars." Jordan was always complaining that ever since Lulu had become successful, nothing about her mom was real anymore—not her hair, not her nails, not her boobs. Not even her name was real. Her real name was Barbara Meyers, but she had it legally changed to Lulu Lavoie after *Lassoed by Lust* was published.

"I wish mine was as long as Juliet DeStefano's," I replied, tugging at my own auburn bob as if that would make it grow faster. No matter how much mousse I put in it, my hair just hung there, like it had just dried after a downpour. "Or at least long enough to put up in a messy bun."

Jordan rolled her eyes. "I bet she wears extensions. My mom had extensions once. They're way nasty."

My eyes widened. "Maybe it's a wig," I gasped. That first day Juliet's hair looked real enough, but it wasn't like I was paying that much attention. "Maybe the witness protection program people bought it for her." I made a mental note to take a closer look next time I was near her.

"Yo, what up, girls?" said a voice behind me as the hand attached to it grabbed for a piece of my donut.

"Hi, Michael," Ali and Jordan said in stereo.

As he leaned in to give me a kiss on the cheek, not even the lemony smell of the dermatologist-prescribed antibacterial soap that he used—which used to make me swoon—did anything. Instead it just reminded me of the stuff our cleaning lady, Marita, used to wax the kitchen floor.

"Hi," I replied, again trying to sound more excited than I felt, which wasn't difficult due to the fact that I felt close to nothing.

Without even asking, he popped the last of my donut into his mouth. "Ready to shop?" he asked, as he took out the travel-size bottle of hand sanitizer he kept in his pocket at all times. After squirting some onto his palm, he held the bottle out to me. "Want some?"

I couldn't help thinking of Dante, and the dirt under his

fingernails. Was a little bit of dirt or Boston cream *that* bad? Didn't traces of dirt or sticky stuff show that you were actually *living* your life? Usually, I would say yes to the sanitizer, but it was time to start living on the edge a little more.

"No thanks," I said. Maybe I wasn't ready to be as rebellious as Devon in *Consumed with Controversy*, when she moved into a tree house to protest the killing of baby seals and ended up falling in love with a CNN anchorman, but not being germfree 24/7 was a step in that direction.

"What about this?" I yelled over the techno music that was thumping away in Always 16 as I held up a zebra-striped tank dress.

"If you want to look like one of those hookers on Hollywood Boulevard," Michael shouted back as he grabbed it from me and put it back on the rack.

Julia Roberts had been a Hollywood Boulevard hooker in *Pretty Woman*, my favorite movie of all time, and she didn't do so bad for herself. But the more I thought about it, Michael was right. Zebra was pretty dramatic. I may have been able to pull off leopard—at least in scarf or headband form—but you had to be Devon Devoreaux or Juliet DeStefano to rock zebra. Plus, after Julia Roberts met Richard Gere, he took her on a huge makeover shopping spree, so she stopped wearing the zebra.

"Here, try this on," Michael said, thrusting a red- and white-flowered sundress into my hand.

27

"Maybe if I were a milkmaid," I replied, putting it back on the rack next to the zebra print.

"Trust me—it'll look great," he said, picking it up again.

I took it from him and started toward the dressing room. The spark may have been gone between us, but I knew better than to fight with him when it came to clothes.

As usual, he was right. Instead of looking babyish, the red and white looked sweet and feminine, and although the dress wasn't fitted, it had this way of making it look like I had some curves under it. I don't know how, but the dress even made my hair look less flat. It was perfect for Miss April.

"Yo, do you have it on?" Michael was yelling from the dressing room entrance. "Let me see."

I walked out and stood in front of him. "Please don't say 'I told you so.'"

"Okay. I won't."

Even Jordan liked it, and for the last year she'd been wearing the unofficial Young Feminist uniform of baggy camouflage pants and T-shirts that said things like WOMYN ROCK.

But it was as we made our way back to the parking lot and came upon a blank-faced, noseless mannequin at the Charlene's Chapeau cart that I discovered the real reason fate had brought me to the Dell that day.

There it was.

A red cowboy hat.

It was the coolest thing I had ever seen. Even cooler than the Indian-inspired sari that Devon had worn on the cover of *Awash in Adventure*.

I ran over and picked it up, cradling it in my hands like a baby chick. "I have to have this," I whispered.

"What are *you* going to do with a red cowboy hat?" came Michael's voice from behind me.

I placed it gently on my head. "Wear it," I replied. It may have been a little big (okay, a *lot* big), but I knew it was just the thing to jump-start my life.

He shook his head. "Nah. You're not a red cowboy hat kinda girl."

Everyone—even the donut guy—seemed to think they knew who I was. Or, rather, who I *wasn't*. According to them, I wasn't a Dark as Midnight girl, I wasn't a Boston cream girl, I wasn't a zebra girl. Maybe the good-grade-getting, always-home-before-curfew, finish-all-her-vegetables Sophie wouldn't wear or eat any of that stuff, but the *real* me would. It was time to stop hiding my true self and finally show people the wild and dramatic side of me—and a red cowboy hat was the perfect way to start.

"I am so a red cowboy hat kind of girl!" I cried. I decided to leave out that Dante had bought Devon one *exactly* like it when, after finally getting bored of making mad, passionate love, they got out of bed and went into town in search of food. Except hers had purple feathers hanging off it, while mine—or the one that would soon be mine—was feather-free and more classic and understated.

The bored, iPod-wearing guy at the cart handed me a mirror to check myself out. "I knew it!" I gasped. "It's perfect." Not only would it look great with my new dress in the calendar, but it was the thing that I knew would transform my life and finally make me feel like I was really living!

"Come on—take it off. You look stupid," Michael said impatiently.

"I do not," I snapped. Maybe he didn't appreciate it, but surely my two best friends would. I turned to them. "Isn't it just perfect?"

Ali shrugged. "You look like one of those waitresses in that barbecue place on Pico Boulevard."

Imagination was not Ali's strong suit. What did I expect from someone who was in AP calculus as a junior?

"I was thinking more like the people behind the counter at Arby's," Jordan said. Not only did I need a new boyfriend, but I could've used some new friends as well. Jordan, Ali, and I had been BFFs for a long time, but sometimes I wondered if the reason they dissed all my ideas was because they were trying to hold me back. Like they were worried that if my life became as dramatic and exciting as it was destined to be, I'd leave them behind.

I turned to the cart guy. "How much is it?"

"Sixty-five ninety-nine."

Sixty-five ninety-nine?! For a red cowboy hat?! It wasn't even nice felt.

"Michael's right, Soph," said Jordan. "You're not a red cowboy hat kinda girl."

"But Devon's a red cowboy hat kinda woman!" I cried.

"*Devon isn't real*," the three of them said in unison.

"If I'm not a red cowboy hat kinda girl, what am I then?" I demanded.

"A red- and white-flowered sundress girl?" suggested Michael.

Dante never would have said that to Devon.

Jordan took the hat off my head and placed it back on the mannequin. "Let's go. I just remembered I need to send out an e-mail about the second annual Don't Shave Your Legs Week."

A few carts later, we hit the sunglasses.

"What do you think?" I asked, modeling a pair with huge, oversize lenses.

Ali wrinkled her nose. "You look like some has-been movie star who's just begging to have her picture taken by the paparazzi."

"Yeah," agreed Jordan. "It's like they scream, 'I know I'm trying to look like I don't want you to notice me, but, really, all I want is for you to notice me.'" She took them off my face and examined them. "Actually, I think my mom has the same pair. Except hers are Chanel instead of Chunnel."

I didn't even bother asking Michael his opinion because I knew he'd put the kibosh on them. But I couldn't keep letting these people hold me back—it was time to turn into my best, most dramatic self. First, the red cowboy hat, and now this. "Well, I'm buying them," I said defiantly, reaching into my bag for my wallet. Especially because the sign said they were only fourteen ninety-five.

"Suit yourself," said Michael, "but I bet you end up never wearing them."

Boy, was he wrong. I wore the sunglasses every chance I could—on my way to school, on my way home from school, when I was *at* school and had to go outside and walk to different buildings. I didn't wear them in class because that was in the "Don'ts" section of the *Castle Heights Student Handbook*, but I did wear them inside my house, until I almost broke my toe when I stubbed it on the stairs because the lenses were so dark it made it hard to see.

"Oh, honey—what *fabulous* glasses!" shrieked Lulu when Jordan and I walked into her kitchen on Sunday evening to load up on snacks while we studied for a trig test. I could tell by the amount of ice cream pints, cookie boxes, and potato chip bags littering the counter that Lulu was deep into one of the binges that happened when she was having writer's block.

"Thanks, Lulu," I replied. The one time I had tried to

call her Mrs. Meyers (before the official name change to Lavoie, of course), she had looked at me like I had told her that her knees were fat (she was so sensitive about her knees that she had used one of her royalty checks from *Elevated by Ecstasy* to pay for liposuction on them).

"I think I have the same ones—they're Chanel, right?" she asked.

"They're *kind* of like Chanel," I replied.

"Except they're kind of *not*," said Jordan, waving her hand around. "Mom, you promised you weren't going to smoke in the house anymore."

Lulu sucked in on her cigarette. "Honey, it's been a stressful day. I had to autograph *one hundred* books for the London Gay Men's Chorus benefit today."

"Well, it reeks," Jordan replied. "Plus, you'll get wrinkles around your mouth."

Unfortunately, it was too late for that. The wrinkles were already there, as was the damage from too many years without sunscreen. Lulu was what my mom referred to as "weathered." But not like dewy, fresh spring weather— more like dry, 115-in-the-shade Palm Springs weather.

"Thank you, my little dermatologist," she replied. "Sophie, I'm so sorry we had to cancel the trip to Mexico." I loved how Lulu always pronounced it the Spanish way: *Me-hee-co*. "When you have to hand a book in every two months, sometimes it's hard to keep all the plots straight. I hope you had time to make other plans."

I gave a long sigh. There was something about being around Lulu that brought out my inner drama queen like nothing else. "Yeah, I have to go to . . . *Florida*."

"*Ooh*, South Beach?" she asked, intrigued.

"No. Delray Beach. To see my grandmother."

Her face fell. "Oh. How—"

"Boring?" I offered.

She shrugged. "Not necessarily. You never know what might happen." A faraway look came over her face. "Who knows—maybe, as you're settling yourself underneath your cashmere throw in your first-class seat, sipping from your complimentary glass of champagne, you'll look up and lock eyes with your seatmate and realize that fate has dealt you a royal flush."

"I'm flying coach, I'm not old enough to drink, and Michael's going to be sitting next to me," I said glumly.

She came out of her trance. "Oh. Hm. Well, maybe at least there'll be a good movie," she said.

"Like something based on a Nicholas Sparks book?" I said hopefully. After Lulu, Nicholas Sparks was my second-favorite author. I owned every one of the movies based on his books on DVD and had watched them so many times they now skipped. Plus, he was massively hot, even if he *was* kind of old and had five kids.

The minute the words came out of my mouth, I regretted them. He was also her biggest competition—even more than Nora Roberts.

"Or, better yet, maybe they'll have one of *your* movies," I said, covering. "Like the made-for-TV version based on *Singed by Secrets*."

She smiled. "Actually, I have a better way for you to spend your vacation." She stood up and started clomping toward her office. "I'll be right back."

"Oh, great," said Jordan, as she made us a tray of snacks: dates, figs, pâté, caviar. At my house, the most exotic thing we had was a papaya once in a while. "I can't wait to see what she comes back with. Maybe she'll lend you her feather-trimmed beach cover-up to wear at the pool."

As Lulu click-clacked back into the kitchen, I immediately saw that what she had in mind was one hundred times *better* than anything sequined or feather-trimmed.

She handed me a book. "Here it is. My latest, and—if I don't say so myself—my greatest yet."

It wasn't just a book. It was an advance reading copy, which meant that it wasn't even available in bookstores yet! "*Propelled by Passion*," I gasped. I squinted at the cover. "Wait a minute. Is that—"

Lulu nodded.

"Oh. My. God. You brought back Dante?!" I squealed.

Jordan put her hands over her ears and winced. "Can we please lose the squealing?"

I looked at the cover again and sighed. There he was: the hottest guy in history, sitting on what looked like a brand-new, top-of-the-line motorcycle, with Devon's arms

35

wrapped around his waist. I loved motorcycles. I hadn't actually been on a real one yet—just one at Magic Mountain, an amusement park—but there was something about the shiny chrome and the earsplitting revving of the engine that drove me wild.

"I know he's your favorite," Lulu said. "Take a look at the dedication."

I opened it. *"For Sophie, whose passion for romance is surpassed only by my own,"* I read aloud. I couldn't believe it—I had a book dedicated to *me*. And not just *a* book, but a book about one of the most incredible heroes in literature. I squinted at the dedication. "Wait a second—it says, 'For Sophir.'"

Lulu took it from me and held it up to her face. "Oh. Huh. Copyeditor screwed up."

Okay, so maybe my name was spelled wrong in the book, but still, I was almost famous. Millions of women around the world would read that and wonder who that Sophie—or Sophir—with a passion for romance was.

"Don't worry—we'll make sure it's fixed when the book goes to print," she added.

I threw my arms around her. "Thank you *soooo* much," I said. "I haven't read it yet, but I already know it's my favorite book ever!" That was a huge compliment coming from someone like me who was such a big reader. I had read the first three Gossip Girl books in one weekend.

Just a few hours before, I had been telling Jordan how

nervous I was to have to sit on a plane for almost seven hours, because I hated flying. But now that I had *Passion* to keep me company, I could have flown to Australia and wouldn't have complained. That being said, Lulu's books were very quick reads because not many of the words were more than three syllables long, so I'd probably be done by the time we were flying over Dante's hometown of Seven Rivers, Montana—which meant I'd either have to read it a second time before we landed, or go back and read *Lassoed by Lust* for the tenth time.

My life may have been boring most of the time, but it was moments like this that made it livable.

"Can you stop looking at that thing for two seconds and focus?" asked Jordan later as we sat in her Indian-slash-hippie-inspired bedroom surrounded by cracker crumbs while some grrl power music played in the background. "We haven't even *touched* cosines yet."

"Huh?" I said, tracing Dante's upper lip and wondering if it was as soft as it looked on the cover.

Jordan took the book from me and tossed it onto the floor. "You can play with that later," she promised, shoving my trig book into my lap.

I turned my head for one more glance at Dante.

"I can't believe I'm best friends with someone who has a crush on a male model who's made a living being objectified," she said.

37

"Objectified" was obviously the Young Feminists' word of the month. The month before, it had been "patriarchal," and the month before that, "subjugated." As in, "Women over the centuries have been subjugated by patriarchal white men," which was a phrase that Jordan tried to work into a conversation whenever she could. Once she managed to bring it up to the Jamba Juice guy, which was pretty impressive. But what was even more impressive was that it turned out that he had been a gender studies major at Harvard, so the comment sparked a long discussion.

I hated when Jordan called Dante a male model. He wasn't. He was . . . Dante, my soul mate. I leaned back on one of the beaded silk pillows on her bed. "Do the Young Feminists of the New Millennium give you a dictionary when you join?" I asked, looking at Dante out of the corner of my eye.

"Very funny," she said. "No, they do not, but I'll tell you this. Last week there was this thread in the forum about how annoying it is when girls put guys before the important things in life—like studying." Her cell phone rang. "Omigod!" she squealed as she looked at the screen. "It's Mark!"

Mark Connor was a senior whom Jordan had had a crush on since the first day of freshman year. Like her, he was really into the idea of trying to change the world, and he was the president of the Go Green, BFFs with the Middle East, and Emo Is Excellent clubs. Up until last fall, he hadn't been sure whether he liked guys or girls, but it seemed from the growing amount of e-mails and texts that he and Jordan had been sending to each other over the last month that he had decided on girls.

She shooed me out of the room. "Go, go! You'll make me nervous if you stay!"

"But what about cosines?" I asked.

"They can wait," she said, shutting the door.

I wandered downstairs and heard the clicking of computer keys coming from Lulu's office. I walked over and stood at the door, which was open a crack. I tried not to breathe too loudly because I knew geniuses hated to be disturbed when they were creating.

As I watched her sprawl out on her cheetah-print chaise lounge, her fingers flying across her laptop keys, stopping every few seconds to take a drag off her cigarette, I wondered if I would ever find something that I was good at that also made me tons of money.

I guess I was breathing louder than I thought, because after a while Lulu looked toward the door and smiled. "Hi, honey. Come on in," she said.

"Oh. I don't want to disturb you from your creative midwifing," I sputtered, my cheeks turning red. In the interview with Lulu that had run on RomanceWriters.com last month, that's how she had referred to her writing: "creative midwifing." A midwife was like a very exotic form of nurse who helped you give birth.

"You're not. I was just e-mailing this guy I met on Soulmates.com," she replied. "He's a carpenter-slash-screenwriter," she said, dreamily. "The screenwriter part I can do without, but I do *love* men who work with their hands."

"Like Dante. *He* works with his hands," I said just as dreamily.

It was hard to believe that someone as successful as Lulu had to go online to meet a guy. Probably because she was so busy writing all the time. According to Jordan, although Lulu had sworn she was only going to do online dating for a month, it was now going on six. When I mentioned it to Mom, she said that it didn't surprise her, because a lot of her own love-addicted patients seemed to be obsessed with Internet dating as well. I don't know why she thought Lulu was an addict. So what if she craved romance? Was that such a horrible thing? I mean, *I* craved romance too. Did that make me an addict as well?

Lulu put her laptop aside and patted the chaise. "Come sit," she ordered.

I balanced myself on the corner and crossed my legs, trying to look as sophisticated as she did—which, in jeans and a Castle Heights sweatshirt, wasn't easy.

My iPhone buzzed in my pocket, and I almost fell off the chaise scrambling to pull it out. "Sorry," I apologized, "you just—"

"—never know if this is going to be the e-mail that

changes your life," finished Lulu. "Is it from a secret admirer professing his love?"

I looked at the screen. "No. It's from Old Navy, announcing an upcoming sale," I replied, disappointed.

"So, how are things with you and Michael?" she asked.

"They're . . . fine," I replied.

Her penciled-in right eyebrow shot up. "Uh oh."

"What?"

"'Fine' is not a good word when it comes to love," she clucked. "In fact, 'fine' is a *four-letter word* when it comes to love."

With brilliant lines like that, it was no wonder why Lulu was one of the greatest writers of the twenty-first century. I gave my own long, hard sigh. "I know." It felt so good to be understood.

"So tell Lulu the Love Doctor what's the matter."

I started fiddling with the leopard-print cashmere blanket on the chaise. "I just . . . I don't know . . . I just . . ." Sometimes when I was filled with chaos and confusion my entire vocabulary went out the window.

"He doesn't make you feel nauseous when you see him, like you're having a panic attack and your heart is going to explode into a thousand pieces because it's beating so hard?"

"Exactly!" I cried. It felt so good to spill my guts. Or, rather, to have Lulu spill my guts for me.

"And sometimes, when he's talking to you, his voice sounds like the teacher from Charlie Brown—you know, *womp-womp-womp*—and instead of listening to what he's saying, you're thinking about whether the size-ten, feather-encrusted mules with the five-inch heels you've been drooling over will still be at Saks if you go back for them?"

"Yes!" I cried. "I mean, no! I mean, *yes*, I'm not listening, but I'm not thinking about shoes. I'm thinking about how I'm going to divide my time studying for my midterms."

"Same thing," she shrugged. She took my hand. "The fact of the matter is that your *heart* isn't in it. You're not *propelled by passion* the way you once were. You're not *insane with lust* like you used to be."

Some people may have found it weird that my best friend's mother talked to me like I was a grown-up, but I was beyond flattered. Obviously, Lulu saw the real me and knew that although I was only sixteen in real time, I was an old soul.

"Well, because I'm only sixteen and still a virgin, I'm not sure I even know what lust feels like, but, yeah, I'm pretty sure that's not in the picture," I replied.

"You want something . . . *more*," Lulu said, twirling her dyed jet-black hair around her Dark as Midnight–painted finger. Even though two of Lulu's nails were broken, they still looked great. "Something . . . *deeper.*"

Listening to her was like listening to this guy I once saw

on an infomercial for "How to Hypnotize a Person and Get Them to Do Whatever You Want, or Your Money Back." "Yes," I agreed dreamily, my eyes fluttering.

"You want to be truly, madly, deeply in love," she said.

I nodded, my eyes now closed as I thought about Dante and his strong arms. Lulu knew exactly how I felt!

I heard the click of the lighter as she lit yet another cigarette. "Yeah, well, good luck. I don't know what to tell you other than if you find a guy that you still feel like that with after the third date, lemme know."

My eyes snapped open so fast I'm surprised they didn't turn inside out. "Huh?" What was the woman who had been crowned the "Queen of Romance" five years in a row talking about?

She exhaled impatiently. "Honey, you *do* know that all that soul mate crap isn't real, right?"

"What?" I said, dazed.

She laughed. "That's just fairy-tale stuff. It doesn't exist."

The thud I heard was my heart hitting the floor. I felt more betrayed than Devon in *Deceived by Deceit*. "But what about your books?" I cried. "That's what you write about better than anyone!" I picked up a copy of *Riddled by Remembrance* and pointed to the back cover. "You're the *Romance Gazette*'s 'best-selling Queen of Romance'—it says so right here!"

As she took a drag off her cigarette, a big piece of ash

fell on her shirt. She shrugged. "I write what people want to read. And people like to read fairy tales. It's not like they want to read about real life. If they wanted that, they'd just read the 'Stars—Just Like Us!' part of *US Weekly*."

"So you don't really believe in love?" I whispered. How could this be? I was crushed. It was like finding out the truth about Santa Claus and the tooth fairy and the Easter bunny in one sitting.

She stubbed out her cigarette. Instead of looking sophisticated, the lipstick marks on the end of the filter now looked disgusting. "Oh, honey, it's not that I don't believe in it. Of *course* I do, or I wouldn't have had to go to that rehab for codependency last year." Romeo, her ancient, half-blind black cat, made his way into the room and bumped over to her lap. She snuggled him to her chest and started petting him. The way the light was hitting her face, I could see the wrinkles through the caked-on makeup on her face. "It's just that that kind of intensity can't sustain itself. Maybe it's there for a few months—or, in my case, a night—but then one morning you wake up and it's just . . . gone." Her face hardened. "And soon enough, you're having these vicious arguments about whether to have Italian or sushi for dinner, but it's not *really* about Italian or sushi—it's about the fact that *yet again*, you've gotten into a relationship that has allowed you to re-create your childhood all over again because he's just as emotionally unavailable and inconsistent as your alcoholic father was," she said bitterly.

I moved back a bit. She was starting to scare me.

She put on the smile that she wore during bookstore signings. "But that's, just, you know, one person's take on it."

I smiled back at her and stood up. It was the same smile I gave the homeless woman who stood outside my neighborhood Starbucks babbling about the fact that she used to be someone back in the seventies when she guest-starred on a sitcom called *One Day at a Time*.

"I should probably get going," I said. "We're having macrobiotic food tonight because it's supposed to cure cancer, even though none of us have cancer." I held up the book. "Thanks again for this."

"Do you want me to autograph it for you?" she asked.

"Oh. I guess so," I replied. What was the point, though? Anything she wrote would just be another vicious lie.

She took the book from me, walked over to her desk, got one of her custom-made pink ink markers that smelled like strawberries, and scribbled something in it.

"Here you go, honey," she said, handing it back to me.

I opened it.

Always remember that you can't go wrong by following your heart.

Best wishes,

Lulu Lavoie

Not only was it a lie, but I knew from looking at the autographed copies in bookstores that that's what she *always* wrote. And the dedication? "Whose passion for romance is surpassed only by my own?" Ha! Lulu didn't believe in love or passion. She just wrote about it so she could buy five-hundred-dollar pairs of shoes! I was seriously considering sending an anonymous e-mail to her publisher to let them know their star writer was actually a fraud.

Lulu may not have believed in earth-shattering, world-rocking, once-in-a-lifetime true love, but *I*, Sophie Rebecca Greene, did. It existed. I knew it.

And I was going to follow my heart and find it.

three

After my conversation with Lulu, I sent Michael a "we need to talk" text. There was no way I could spend a week with him, living a lie, now that I was committed to proving Lulu wrong and finding true love. Everyone on the planet knew that next to "You blew your SATs," "We need to talk" were the four scariest words you could ever hear. Everyone but Michael, that is, because he didn't even bother to respond—which, once Ali came up with her brilliant idea, turned out to be not such a bad thing.

"You should do an Operation Remotivation," Ali panted as Jules, our Pilates teacher, barked orders into her headset microphone for us to squeeze our glutes. This year Castle Heights had started offering Pilates and yoga classes as part of gym class. I thought Pilates would be a piece of cake, which would be good for me since I wasn't a big fan of exercise, but it turned out to be harder than running the six-hundred-yard dash. The only good part about it was that

Juliet DeStefano was in the class, so I got to spend the hour watching her to see if I could pick up any clues about the mysterious past that she was hiding. The way she pulled her hair into a ponytail made me think it wasn't a wig, but what was she whispering in Phan's ear? Was she telling her that the guilt had become too much and she needed to confess that she had accidentally murdered some guy in self-defense when he had been overcome by her beauty and tried to take things too far? Phan's English wasn't very good, so Juliet would've known her secret was safe with her.

"Higher, people! Higher!" screamed Jules into her headset. "The toddlers in the Mommy and Me Pilates class I teach have more stamina than you wimps!"

"What's Operation Remotivation?" I panted back. Hopefully, all this exercise would make me look great for the Miss April photo shoot.

"Okay, people—take five," Jules barked. "Little Andrea over here is having *another* asthma attack."

A class-wide sigh could be heard as we plopped down on our backs.

"When Rachel starts getting on my mother's nerves and it gets to the point where the way she chews her food makes Mom feel like she's going to go postal on her," Ali said, "she has this whole ritual she does to get remotivated about the relationship."

Rachel was Ali's mom's girlfriend. Apparently, it didn't matter if you were straight *or* gay—every relationship seemed doomed. "Yeah, my mom does the same thing," I said. "Except she calls it 'withdrawing projections and loving the person for who they are, rather than who you want them to be.'"

Ali wrinkled her nose. "Huh?"

I shrugged. "It's shrink talk," I replied. I stood up as nonchalantly as possible and arranged myself into a half-yoga, half-Twister-like move.

"What are you doing?" asked Ali.

"Trying to check out what Juliet's doing," I whispered.

Ali squinted. "She's just sitting there biting her cuticles."

"It may *look* like that's what she's doing," I said, "but I bet what she's really doing is deciding whether to turn herself in."

"Turn herself in for what?" Ali asked, confused.

"Forget it," I said. "So back to Operation Remotivation. What exactly does your mom do?"

"Well, first she makes a list of all the good things about Rachel—you know, about how she's smart, funny, pretty, a good listener, not a psychopath like Lisa, her last girlfriend. And then she plans a special evening—takes off her base-ball cap and blow-dries her hair, wears a dress instead of yoga pants, lets Rachel win at Scrabble."

I could do that. Although it would be Wii bowling instead of Scrabble. And if I let Michael win, I'd never hear the end of it.

"She says there's this prayer she learned in yoga called the St. Francis prayer: 'It's better to love, than be loved, give than receive.'" Ali went on. "It's like that Buddhism stuff about getting rid of your ego and helping other people."

"I guess it can't hurt," I agreed. At this point anything was worth a try. Although it was hard to remember, once upon a time, Michael and I had had that same deep connection that Devon and Dante did. I'd hate to find out from a psychic years from now that Michael was my eternal soul mate and I wasted an entire lifetime not being with him.

That night, after watching the *Top 100 Craziest Femme Fatales* special that I had TiVo'd on SOAPnet (I'm sorry, but Sydney from *Melrose Place* so deserved to be in the top five rather than number thirteen), I made a list.

I wrote *Michael Rosenberg: Pros* at the top of my notebook paper.

1. Funny (but thinks he's funnier than he actually is)

2. Good kisser (but have not kissed anyone else other than Toby Braverman a.k.a. Camp Guy when I was twelve, and that was only for three seconds, so not sure if he's *actually* good or if it's just because I don't have any other reference)

3.   Excellent taste in clothes (even though he doesn't think I should wear dramatic accessories such as red cowboy hats or fake Chanel sunglasses because they're quote-unquote not me)

4.   Jeremy loves him

Then I wrote *Michael Rosenberg: Cons* on the next page.

1.   Love, but not *in* love with him

2.   Interrupts a lot

3.   Love, but not *in* love with him

4.   Calls, but then doesn't have anything to say and doesn't pay attention

5.   Talks like he's a rapper

6.   Love, but not *in* love with him

7.   Won't share his fries because he says he has issues with people's hands near his food. But he doesn't have a problem taking any of *my* fries

8.   Love, but not *in* love with him

9. Says "I told you so" a lot

10. Love, but not *in* love with him

I could have kept going, but I figured that was enough. I sure was glad there was a second half to Operation Remotivation. Otherwise, I would have had to break up with Michael immediately.

I picked up my cell and pushed his name on speed dial.

"Yo, what up? It's not nine yet," he said when he answered.

"I know. I just . . . missed you so much, I couldn't stop myself from picking up the phone and calling you." Okay, so it was kind of a lie, but it felt like a remotivating thing to say.

"Oh. Well, thanks. So, what's up?" was his reply.

I cringed as he did #5 on the "Cons" list. "Nothing. How are you?"

The only response was the blare of the TV in the background.

"Michael?"

"Huh?"

"I said, how are you?"

"Fine."

I waited for him to go on, but he didn't. I made a mental note to add "doesn't like to chitchat" to my list.

"Oh, and in addition to missing you, I wanted to see if you wanted to come over tomorrow night," I said.

"For what?"

"To hang out."

"With you and Jeremy?"

"No. Just with me," I replied. "Tomorrow night is the Asperger's support group."

"Oh," he said. "Okay. I guess so."

He sounded as if he was about to get a cavity filled.

"You don't want to hang out alone with me?"

There was a pause. "Of course I do."

Dante once told Devon that being apart from her was as painful as when he had an impacted wisdom tooth. Was it too much to ask for a boyfriend who felt that way about *me*? I made another mental note to add "no interest in making out when parents aren't home" to the list.

I decided to go all out. "I was thinking I'd get us some sushi," I said. Even if I had to go behind my mother's back and use a month's worth of allowance.

"Sushi?" he perked up. "From Nozawa?"

I sighed. If only Michael got as excited about me as he did about an inside-out yellowtail roll, we wouldn't be in this situation. "Uh huh," I said.

"Okay," he replied.

"Good. Want to say six thirty?" I asked.

"Sure."

"Well, I guess I'll see you tomorrow then."

"Okay. Bye," he said as he hung up.

My heart sank. I thought back to the night a few years before when we stayed on the phone so long we both fell asleep mid-conversation and woke up to find our batteries had died. Why couldn't it be like that again? Grandma Roz was always saying, "The only constant is change," but why couldn't just the bad things change and get good? Why did the good things have to change too?

I picked up *Propelled by Passion* and started tracing Dante's biceps. "Oh, Dante," I sighed. "Why can't you be real and ten years younger and not a male model?"

Jeremy hated the Asperger's support group meetings ("How would you like to spend two hours surrounded by people who won't look you in the eye and who spout random facts about things you don't care about?" he'd say to me every time I tried to get him excited about it), which is why Mom and Dad always tried to bribe him by taking him to the Olive Garden for dinner first. As soon as they left the house at five o'clock, I went up to my parents' bathroom and started a bath. I had a bathtub in my bathroom, but I figured it would help get me in the right mood if I took a bubble bath in the big sunken tub. Because it was a special occasion, I decided to use some of Mom's expensive bath oil.

There's no way Michael's going to be able to resist me now, I thought as I slid into the tub. Especially because the oil was called Irresistible. Just to make sure, I used three quarters of the bottle. That probably explained why, as I reached for a washcloth, my butt slid on the bottom of the tub and my head ended up underwater.

"Whoops," I sputtered when I was upright again.

"What'd you do—wash your hair with vegetable oil?" Jordan asked when she and Ali showed up with the sushi and I emptied out my "Savings Fund for Unnecessary, yet Wildly Dramatic Accessories" that I kept in a shoebox in my closet.

"Is it that bad?" I asked, running my hand through it. I didn't have to work hard; my hand just slid right through.

"Um—" Ali said.

"—kind of," Jordan finished.

Ali sniffed. "How much perfume did you put on?"

"Just a few sprays," I said. I held my wrist out to Jordan. "Do you like it? It's my mom's. It's called Eau de Desire."

"Well, on its own I bet it wouldn't be that bad, but mixed with the bath stuff, it kind of gives off a Lysol smell," Jordan said.

"Um, you guys? You're really not helping here," I said. "This is Operation Remotivation—not Operation Make-Me-Want-to-Stick-My-Head-in-an-Oven-Before-He-Gets-Here."

"You know why Sylvia Plath stuck her head in an oven?" Jordan asked. "Because she knew that no matter what, her stupid poet husband was always going to be seen as the talented one. Because that's the kind of evil, patriarchal society we live in!"

Ali and I ignored her and started cleaning up the family room. The good thing about Jeremy having Asperger's was that he was a neat freak, so, really, all we had to do was straighten the piles of *Psychology Today*s (Mom's), *Golf Digest*s (Dad's), and *TV Guide*s (Jeremy's).

"What is that?" I asked as Ali took a bottle out of her knapsack and started spritzing it around the room.

"It's an essential oil thing called Nights of Passion. You spray it, and it's supposed to," she looked at the label and read, "'magnetize your beloved to you.' I stole it from my mom's night table drawer."

I wrinkled my nose. "It smells like the locker room at school."

Ali shrugged. "You only get one chance at Operation Remotivation."

"You're right," I agreed. "Keep spritzing."

It was already six fifteen by the time we had finished straightening and spritzing and putting some baby powder in my hair in hopes of soaking up some of the oil (a trick Jordan had read in *Allure* back before she had become a Young Feminist). After Jordan and Ali left, I brought my iPod down and cued up my "Best Romantic Songs Ever" playlist. I usually only played it when I was reading Lulu's books, but tonight I needed all the help I could get.

At six thirty the doorbell rang. That was another thing

about Michael—he was always on time. I used to love that about him because I felt like it meant he didn't want to miss a single moment with me, but now it really took away the mystery. For instance, in *Leveled by Longing*, it drove Devon insane with passion when the Brazilian samba dancer would say he'd call her right back and then she wouldn't hear from him for weeks.

"Yo, what up?" Michael asked when I opened the door.

I tried not to cringe. Would I fall back in love with him if he talked normally? And didn't he realize a HIP-HOP HEEB T-shirt was so not sexy?

"What happened to your hair?" he asked.

"I got a little bath oil in it," I replied.

As he walked in, he started sneezing. "Are you wearing perfume?"

I nodded. "A little."

"Why? You never wear perfume."

I shrugged. "It's a special occasion."

"What's the occasion?"

Obviously, I couldn't tell him that the special occasion was Operation Remotivation. "Never mind."

I started toward him to give him a kiss, but before I could do it, he walked into the family room and plopped down on the couch with the remote.

I moved in front of the screen. "So what do you think of the dress?" I asked, modeling it.

He kept clicking the remote. "I like it," he said, barely looking at me. "Remember, I helped you pick it out?"

When he stopped clicking, I turned around to see what he was watching. A girl with blonde cornrows was shaking her butt in a music video.

"Do you think she's pretty?" I asked.

He shrugged. "I don't know. She's okay, I guess." But from the way he kept leaning to the right to see the screen, it was clear he thought she was more than okay. Was that the problem? Did he want a hoochie mama instead of a nice Jewish girl like me? Finally, he tore his eyes away from the TV. "Did you get the sushi?"

"Yeah."

"Can we eat it in here? *Best Rap Videos of the Last Decade* is on at seven."

"I was thinking we could eat in the dining room," I replied. "I have a surprise for you."

"What is it?" he asked.

"If I told you, it wouldn't be a surprise, would it?"

"I guess," he said, standing up. "So can we eat now? I'm starved."

"Yeah. But wait a second." I reached into my pocket and took out a tie that I had borrowed from my dad's closet. "First, you have to put this on."

"You want me to wear a *tie* to eat sushi?"

"No. You have to wear it as a blindfold," I said, as I put it around his eyes.

58

"You're crazy," he said.

I took his arm and started leading him to the dining room. "Crazy about you," I replied, which is what Dante always said to Devon.

He stopped and lifted the tie off of his left eye to look at me. "What has gotten into you?"

I ignored him and kept leading (more like yanking) him to the dining room. When we arrived, I removed the tie. "So what do you think?" I said excitedly.

I had taken every candle I could find in the house and put them on the table. Because there were about twenty of them, lighting them had been a huge pain in the butt—especially since I had singed the tips of my hair a few times in the process. The way I had taken all the pieces of sushi and edamame and put them in the shape of little hearts gave it a superromantic effect. I would have liked to be able to take credit for the idea, but the truth was Dante had done the same thing for Devon, except instead of sushi, he had used Hot Tamales.

"It looks cool," he replied. "But you don't think any of the wax dripped on the sushi, do you?"

That was it. It was too much. I tried to hold it together, but like Devon, I had a passionate nature that made it difficult to hide my emotions at times—especially when I was PMSing, which I was. As I sat there watching Michael inspect a piece of spicy tuna for candle wax, I burst into tears.

He looked up from the sushi, confused. "What's the matter?"

Operation Remotivation was a bust. It wasn't working. It was *never* going to work. At least not with Michael. I realized that the moment to have The Talk had arrived. To tell Michael that as much as I loved him, I wasn't *in* love with him, and because of that, we should probably go our separate ways—which is what Devon had told the hippie rain forest activist she had met in Costa Rica in *Riddled by Remembrance.*

But I just . . . couldn't. Literally. Because when I opened my mouth to tell him, I choked on the mint I had been sucking on to make sure I had minty-fresh breath when we kissed. When I could breathe again, I started crying again.

"Why are you crying?" he asked, puzzled.

"I'm not," I said, wiping my eyes. "I mean, I *was*, a second ago, but now I'm not. Now I'm just sniffling. I think I'm just PMSing."

He put down the sushi and walked over and gave me a hug. Michael's kisses no longer set my loins aflame with passion, as Devon would say, but he *did* give awesome hugs. He used just the right amount of pressure. "I'm sorry," he said as he squeezed me.

How was I going to give that up? I started to cry again.

"What's the matter now?" he asked.

"Nothing. I'm fine," I said, willing myself to buck up.

After a few more squeezes, he let go of me. "You sure you're okay?"

I nodded as I swiped at my eyes some more.

"Good. Do you want to go fix your makeup?"

"Why?" I sniffled.

"I don't know. Because you look a little bit like a raccoon?" he suggested.

I could tell he was trying to be helpful, but it didn't stop me from bursting into tears again.

"You don't have to," he said, patting me again. "I just thought, you know, you might want to, before we eat. Not because it would gross me out or anything while I was eating, but because, you know, you have such pretty eyes."

I started crying harder. This was why I was so *confused*. What was I supposed to do when he went and said something so romantic?

"I'll be right back," I sniffled as I walked toward the bathroom.

After I splashed some cold water on my face and ruined one of my mom's good guest towels with mascara streaks, I stared at myself in the mirror. "Why are you throwing away something so rare and precious?" I said to my greasy-haired, puffy-eyed reflection in the mirror. "Michael *loves* you. Maybe he only said it once, on your fifteenth birthday, because you refused to let him have that second piece of cake unless he did, but that's just because, like a lot of guys, he has trouble

61

talking about his feelings." I blew my nose. "Millions of girls would *kill* to have someone like him," I said. Okay, maybe not *millions* of girls—maybe just Annie Bellamy, who went to Buckley, his high school, with him and always freaked me out when I saw her because last year she had gotten into Wicca and I was afraid she was going to put a spell on me.

When I walked back to the dining room, I found that Michael had blown out the candles and moved the sushi to the family room, where he was watching *Celebrity Rehab with Dr. Drew* on VH1.

"Is this cool?" he asked with his mouth full of yellowtail.

"Sure," I sighed, plopping down next to him and plucking a piece of freshwater eel off the plate.

We spent the rest of the evening like we usually did— stuffing our faces while Michael channel surfed.

Operation Remotivation was a bust, but the second red velvet cupcake that I let myself have for dessert helped soften the blow a *little* bit.

four

Friday was the first of April, a.k.a. Horoscope Day. I can't stand being late, so Thursday night I had to set my alarm for fifteen minutes earlier than usual so that when I woke up I could log on to HoroscopeAddicts.com and still make it out the door at exactly 7:16 a.m. That would get me to school anywhere between seven and nine minutes before the first bell rang. There were a lot of great astrology columns on there—Alistair Allbright's "Destiny Awaits You" and Natasha Romanoff's "The View from Venus," for instance—but my favorite was one called "The Stars Never Lie" by a little old Irish woman named Wanda McManus. From the picture on her site, Wanda looked to be about seventy-five, and the "About Wanda" page said that she was descended from a long line of astrologers and psychics and had a bit of faerie in her from her mother's side as well.

The reason I liked Wanda so much was because, like

me and Devon, she was a true romantic. Instead of focusing on money and career stuff, her horoscopes talked only about love and soul mates and the best days of the month for falling in love and meeting your soul mate. For $24.95, she also did personalized compatibility charts. Last year I had used some of my birthday money to get mine and Michael's done. It had said that we were indeed soul mates, but that "fate would first deal us a myriad of twists and turns and trials and tribulations that would need to be conquered before we could live in eternal bliss." That seemed fair enough. Except that I then used the rest of my birthday money to get my compatibility chart with Dante done. (I'm not *crazy*—I mean, I know he's not a real person or anything like that—but Lulu had once written that his birthday was December 5th and I wanted to see how we would have matched up had he actually *existed*.) It ended up saying the same exact thing, except that instead of "twists and turns and trials and tribulations" it said "trials and tribulations and twists and turns."

I had also noticed that the seventh and the seventeenth seemed to always be listed as the "Best Days for Love This Month," and the month of April was no different. The seventh was the day that Michael and I were flying to Florida, so I'm not sure how romantic that could be, but it also said that the seventh was a new moon solar eclipse, which I knew from my horoscope research was a *very* dramatic thing as it only happened a few times a year.

What Wanda *didn't* put in April's monthly column was, "On the fifth, your entire world as you know it will start to come crashing down."

The day started with Michael's mom calling to say that the bugbite he complained about before going to sleep the night before had turned into full-blown chicken pox. Obviously, he wasn't going to Florida.

"So I guess this means I'll have to cancel the trip, right?" I asked hopefully after Mom hung up with her.

"Of course not," she said, as she started to wipe the counter, pour some pomegranate juice for Jeremy, and cut up some cantaloupe for me (Mom: Lots of vitamin A to help with poor eyesight. Me: But I have 20/20 vision. Mom: *Exactly*—because you eat your cantaloupe!). "Why would you have to cancel?"

I shrugged. "I don't know. Because I can't carry both candelabras by myself?"

"Well, Daddy will just have to wrap them up and pack them in a box with peanuts, and you'll check it," she replied. She put her hands on her hips. "You're going. You don't know how much more quality time you have to spend with your grandmother."

"But you're always saying she's in perfect health!" I cried.

"She is, but you never know. Plus, we decided last night to send Jeremy to your cousin's for the week, which means it'll be the first time your father and I will be alone in years—and I am *not* giving that up."

Little did I know that forty-eight hours later I'd be very grateful to get out of town—even if it was to an old people's village in Florida.

That night, as I was figuring out what to pack, Michael called.

"We need to talk," he said. He must have been really sick, because the TV was off.

I put down my bathing suit. Wait a minute. "We need to talk" was *my* line! "About what?" I asked. I could feel the color drain from my face.

"About us," Michael replied. "But I think we should do this in person. Can you come over?"

In person?! It was getting *worse*.

"But you have chicken pox."

"Yeah, I know. I was thinking you could stand outside my door or something."

"Michael, I am *not* driving over to your house and standing outside your door," I huffed. "If you have something to say to me, say it right now."

"Forget it then," he replied.

That was like waving a red flag in front of a bull. How could a person just forget a "we need to talk" situation?

"You want to *what*?!" I yelped twenty minutes later as I sat outside Michael's bedroom door.

"I want to push the pause button on our relationship," came his muffled response from the other side.

"You're breaking up with me?" I cried. How could this be happening when I was the one who had spent the last few weeks tortured with tumult about breaking up with *him*?

"No," he said. "I told you—I just want to push the pause button."

"Michael, I'm not a . . . DVD player!" I cried. "You can't just turn a person on and off like that!"

"I didn't say I wanted to turn it off and push eject," he said calmly. "I just want to push the pause button. Look, Sophie, you're awesome, but three years with someone at our age is a long time. Percentagewise, it's—can you do the math on your calculator?"

I took out my iPhone. "Eighteen point seventy-five percent of our lives." Wow, that *was* a lot. Had I just wasted my life with the wrong person? I'd be seventeen next January—it wasn't like I was a kid anymore.

"I just want to, I don't know, see what else is out there. You know, try another station at the buffet. Being so sick has made me think about a lot of things," he said.

"You have *chicken pox*, Michael," I replied. "Not cancer."

"My fever was all the way up to one oh two point seven at one point!" he said defensively.

I stood up. It was depressing enough that I now had to spend an entire week alone with my grandmother, choking

67

on the fumes of Bengay mixed with stewed prunes. I didn't need to sit on the floor while my on-pause boyfriend told me he wanted to see if anything better was out there.

"Good-bye, Michael," I said to the door. "I hope . . . I hope you spend the week really, really itchy!" I huffed before stomping down the stairs and out to the car.

As I stopped short at a yellow light (I had seen enough videos in Drivers Ed to know you were just setting yourself up for major tragedy by going through one), I realized that maybe Michael semi-breaking up with me was just the "manicured hands of fate," as Lulu called them, in action. Once they announced the calendar winners the next morning and I became Miss April, my life was going to take off so fast that even if I *had* still been in love with him, our love probably wouldn't have been able to survive.

It always took Mrs. Anton, our principal, a long time to get through the morning announcements because of her stutter, but the next morning it seemed to take *extra* long.

"And now," she finally said, "French club president Michelle Goldman has some important news about the first annual French club calendar that will be available for purchase next fall."

"*Merci beaucoup*, Madame Anton," Michelle said. "And *merci* to everyone at Castle Heights who took the time to e-mail their suggestions about which Castle Heights students they think best embody each month of the year. And now, it is *avec plus de plaisir* that I announce the winners. For Miss January, we have Juliet DeStefano!"

What?! Juliet DeStefano wasn't even *in* the French club!

"For Miss February, Juliet DeStefano."

My mouth fell open so wide that my gum fell out and landed on my desk.

"March—Juliet again!" she continued.

What was going on?! Had Juliet *bribed* Mrs. Anton or Michelle? For someone with such a shady past, I wouldn't put it past her. That being said, April had to be mine.

"April—*quelle surprise!* Juliet DeStefano!" Michelle announced. I put my head down on the desk.

Quelle surprise, it turned out that Juliet was also going to be Miss May through December as well. Instead of being the French Club of Castle Heights High Calendar, it had become the Juliet-DeStefano-in-Twelve-Different-Outfits Calendar. Kids who sit in the middle of the cafeteria aren't really the type to protest like, say, Wally Twersky, who was always staging sit-ins or stand-ins or lie-ins or stuff like that. And I was never one to rock the boat. But before I knew it, all that passion that had spent the last sixteen years steeping inside me, like the herbal sun tea that my mom made in summer, spilled out. As soon as the bell rang, instead of turning right and going to history, I turned left and marched straight toward the office so I could catch Michelle.

"*Bonjour*, Sophie, *ça va?*" she said as she walked out of Mrs. Anton's office wearing a beret and her blue and white boatnecked shirt. Mademoiselle Fritsche, our French club advisor who had lived in Paris for four years, said that no one wore those shirts except for dumb American tourists.

"Don't *ça va* me, Michelle," I growled. "You do realize that what just happened went completely against school rules?"

"What are you talking about?" she asked.

"This is a calendar to raise money for the French club!" I cried. "Juliet DeStefano isn't even *in* the French club! She's not in *any* clubs!" Probably because she didn't want to risk her past catching up with her if anyone got hold of our yearbook.

"I don't remember us voting on a motion that said it was limited to French club members only," she said.

"That's because that part was *understood*!" I cried. "And who voted for her? Other than Phan, she doesn't have any friends!"

"Probably the entire male student body," she replied.

I guess she was right. "Well, I have it on good authority that I happened to get a lot of votes for the month of April," I said.

"Okay, Sophie. As president of the French club, I certainly wouldn't want there to be any sort of controversy during my administration, so I'll talk to Miss Fritsche about this *tout de suite* and get back to you."

"Thank you," I said, and turned on my heel.

"*Au revoir!*" she cried after me as I stomped down the hall.

I know I had wanted drama, but this was ridiculous. Between Michael and this calendar, I was feeling a little sick to my stomach.

Which, by the end of lunch, had turned into *a lot* sick.

I wished I was a stoner or a goth or a video-game geek and sat on the fringes at lunch, because even though I may have felt invisible, that day I sure wasn't.

I was eating my smoked turkey and Swiss sandwich when Michelle sauntered over. "*Bonjour*, Sophie. *Ça va?*" she asked.

This was no time for small talk. I put down my sandwich. "Did you talk to Miss Fritsche?" I demanded.

"I did. And she agreed with me that by limiting the calendar just to French club students we'd risk being seen as elite and discriminating. *Quel dommage*," she said, which meant, "What a pity."

It figured. "Well, thanks anyway," I sighed.

As she walked away, Ali shook her head. "I can't believe you voted for yourself *fifty-four* times with all those fake e-mail addresses and you *still* didn't get Miss April!" she said.

"Shhh," I said. Her older brother was partially deaf because he was a metalhead, so Ali tended to talk really loud. Her whispers were more like regular people's yells.

71

Unfortunately, luck would have it that Kyra Mattson was sitting right behind us that day. Not only did Kyra have supersonic bionic hearing, but she was also a huge gossip. By the time I got to history later that afternoon, a group of kids were gathered around Matt Rabinov's iPhone, laughing.

"What's so funny?" I asked.

"You're the latest entry in UrbanDictionary.com," said Hannah Brodsky.

"What are you talking about?" I said, pushing my way through the crowd so I could see.

"*Sophie Greene (n.) A person who tries to rig an election but fails miserably,*" it said on the screen. "*e.g., 'Dude, whatever you do, don't try and pull a Sophie Greene unless you want to commit social suicide.'*"

Oh. My. God. Why couldn't this have happened last period when I was in chemistry and could've downed some hydrochloric acid right then and there? Needless to say, I kept my head down the rest of the day and tried to ignore the snickers.

Thank god it was the last day before break.

As I walked through the Dell after school toward Nordstrom to buy the SPF 85 sunblock that Mom insisted I wear, I wondered how I was ever going to show my face at school again. I had wanted to be noticed, but not like *this*. Thankfully, I had a whole week before I had to go back, but maybe I'd just stay in Florida forever. I could get a job as a checkout girl at the Publix supermarket or become a wait-ress at Red Robin and rake in the tips during the early bird dinner shift. Sure, it wasn't New York or Paris or London, but at least I wouldn't have to worry about people star-ing at me, if only because they couldn't see me since they were old and almost legally blind.

Until then, though, I needed something to help me go incognito. Yes, school was out, but I still had to suffer through twelve more hours in L.A., and the idea of run-ning into someone I knew sounded as painful as watching Jeremy suffer through a birthday party with non-Asperger kids.

Then I had a moment of brilliance just before I got to Nordstrom. I stopped and turned around. Luckily, I knew just the thing.

"Sixty-seven, sixty-eight, sixty-nine, seventy!" I said to the cart guy as I counted out the bills. "You can even keep the five cents." I placed the red cowboy hat on my head. It was just as dramatic looking as I remembered. Even though it was still too big, I could feel my entire DNA change as I strode back to the car. Not only that, but when I passed by Dylan Schoenfield and heard her talking about the Urban Dictionary thing with Amy Loubalu (I couldn't believe the news had made it all the way to the seniors), they totally didn't recognize me.

I may not have been Miss April, and I may have been

semi-dumped the night before, but with every step, I could feel myself getting closer to my destiny.

"All set?" Mom asked the next morning when I came down to the kitchen with my carry-on. She, Dad, and Jeremy were waiting to take me to the airport three hours before takeoff. Just once I wish I could have gotten there really late like Devon always did and gotten a special escort to whisk me through security, but as long as my parents were involved, that was never going to happen. I mean, sure, I didn't like being late, and so I understood getting there an hour early, or two hours early for an international flight, but three?

"Yes, I'm all set," I said.

"You have your vitamins?"

I nodded.

"Copies of medical records in case of emergency?"

I nodded again.

"Maxi pads?"

"Mom!"

"What?"

I gestured toward Dad and Jeremy. "Um, males in the room?"

She shrugged. "Your grandmother went through menopause years ago. I want you to be prepared."

"Yes, I packed my maxi pads," I sighed.

"Sunblock?"

I hesitated. "Yes." A lie, I know. At least it wasn't a *huge* one, like when Devon "forgot" to tell the English prime minister that she was married to someone else before she agreed to marry him in *Frazzled with Forgetting*. I'd buy some sunblock at the Garden of Eden pharmacy.

"What about the lox and whitefish?" Dad asked.

"What lox and whitefish?" I asked, confused.

"Oh my God! I can't believe we almost forgot the lox and whitefish!" exclaimed Mom as she rushed toward the fridge.

"Mom didn't tell you?" said Dad. "Grandma Roz wants lox and whitefish from Nate 'n Al's." Nate 'n Al's was one of the oldest delis in L.A.

"You want me to bring *fish* on an *airplane*?" I said. "That's going to reek!"

He sighed. "What do you want me to tell you? Apparently, it's one of her dying wishes."

"But she's not dying!" I exclaimed. "And there's like four delis within walking distance where she can get that stuff."

He shrugged. "She says none of them hold a menorah candle to Nate 'n Al's."

Mom held out two stinky packages wrapped in white paper. "Here. You can put it in your carry-on—"

"But—"

"But what?"

As I hadn't told Mom and Dad I was a red cowboy hat kinda girl yet, I had put it in my carry-on for the moment.

"Nothing," I said, placing the packages carefully inside my bag. I just hoped the smell of fish wouldn't take away from any of the glamour of my new look.

As Grandma Roz also liked to say, "It's always something."

five

Two hours later, carry-on stowed safely in the overhead compartment, I was settled on American Airlines Flight 121 from Los Angeles International Airport to West Palm Beach. I knew that once I graduated from college and began living a jet-set life, I was going to have to get over my fear of flying, but for now, my hands were clutching the armrests, and my eyes were tightly closed even though we hadn't taken off yet.

"It looks like we're seatmates," I heard a voice say.

I opened my eyes to see an old lady wearing a "San Fernando Valley Knitting Club" sweatshirt and holding a carry-on that didn't look like it was going to fit beneath her seat. *And* an oversize, needlepoint tote bag with a picture of a cat playing with a ball of yarn on it. *And* a patent leather pocketbook.

"My name is Harriet. I'm in 12A," she said pleasantly, pointing at the window.

I nodded. "Sophie. 12C. Nice to meet you."

"You're not blind, dear, are you?"

"Huh?"

She pointed to my Chunnels.

"Oh. No. I just . . ." I thought about telling her I was going incognito in case I ran into any of my classmates (Florida, at least for those of us who were Jewish, was a big Spring Break destination), but announcing you were incognito kind of ruined the point. While I did take the glasses off, I kept my hat on. It was a little crumpled after being folded up in my bag for the ride to the airport, but thankfully, it didn't smell too fishy.

"So, would you mind getting up so I can sneak in there?" she asked. "Back when I was your age, I was a real slimster and probably could've weaseled myself right by you, but that was a long time ago," she chuckled. Judging from the size of her butt in her polyester elastic waistband pants, it had been a very long time ago.

"Sure. Sorry," I said, finally letting go and standing up.

As Harriet wriggled her way through the narrow space in our row, I heard what sounded like a meow coming from the overly large carry-on.

"Excuse me," I said politely, pointing at the carry-on. "Is there a cat in there?"

She looked down at it, where the one meow had now turned into a bunch of nonstop meows, and then looked up at me and smiled. "There sure is," she said proudly. She lifted up a Velcro flap and shoved the case toward me. Through the mesh I could see the shadow of something very large and white, which began to hiss. "This is Lord Byron," she said.

I gasped. "You named your cat after the greatest love poet in history? How cool!" I hadn't actually *read* any of his poems, but one of the prison guards in *Battered by Betrayal*, the one where Devon was thrown in jail after she broke up with a Venezuelan dictator, used to read his poetry to Devon.

"I sure did," Harriet said proudly. "After Nora Roberts, Lord Byron is my favorite writer."

She settled herself in her seat and set Lord Byron between us on 12B. "I'm just going to keep him here until our other seatmate arrives."

"Actually, my boyfriend was 12B, but he's not coming because he has chicken pox," I explained before sneezing. *And because he pushed the pause button,* I thought to myself. Maybe I'd tell Harriet about that later. Because she was old, I bet she had some wisdom she could share with me.

"Oh heavens. I'm so sorry to hear that, but maybe that means Lord Byron is in luck," she chuckled.

I sneezed again.

"You're not allergic to cats, are you?" Harriet asked.

"Uh huh," I got out before sneezing again.

She fished around in her handbag and pulled out a box

of pills and handed it to me. "Here, take one of these," she said.

"What is it?" I asked suspiciously.

"Benadryl. It'll stop you from sneezing."

I made sure to read the entire box—especially the CAUTION! paragraph—to make sure it didn't say anything like, "Do not take if you recently drank a Frappuccino," or something along those lines. A person could never be too careful. As I pushed one of the pills out of the foil wrapper and washed it down with my bottle of water, Lord Byron's meowing got louder and louder.

Harriet sniffed. "Do you smell fish?"

"Uh . . . no," I said nervously. I was glad my carry-on was in the overhead compartment and not underneath my seat, or else Lord Byron *really* would've been yowling.

A few minutes later I dozed off, thanks to the Benadryl—that is, until I was awoken by the arrival of the new tenant of 12B. Not only was he the hottest guy I had ever seen in person, but as I stood up to let him get to his seat, our arms touched and I immediately knew we were soul mates.

After he was settled and I was wracking my brain for something flirty to say, he reached for my book. "*Propelled by Passion*," he read. "Is this any good?"

I shrugged, hoping my face wasn't too red. "I don't know. I just grabbed it off the shelf in the terminal bookstore so I'd have something to read."

"But it says here that it's an 'advance reading copy' and it isn't coming out until June," he replied.

I grabbed the book back and shoved it in my purse. "Really? How weird."

"Can I see it for one more sec?" he asked.

I fished it back out and handed it to him.

"He looks kind of familiar to me," he said, squinting. Omigod—I had no idea a squint could be so *sexy*. "Wait a minute—we kind of look alike, don't you think?"

I pretended to examine the cover as if I hadn't spent hours already doing so. I hoped there weren't smudge marks from where I had kissed it. "I don't know . . . maybe a little."

He turned to me all excited. "Hey, do you think it's true when they say that everyone has a twin?"

"You mean a doppelgänger?" piped up Harriet.

The two of us turned to her. I was so busy falling in love that I had nearly forgotten all about Harriet and Lord Byron, even though he was now yowling at full volume. I guess that's what Devon had meant when she said that the world fell away when she met Dante.

The Hot Guy sat up straight. "What's a doppelgänger, ma'am?" he asked, all polite.

He was nice to old people! I *loved* that. "Yeah. What's a doppelgänger?" I echoed. I loved that we didn't know the same words.

"Well, literally translated from the German, it means

'double-goer,'" Harriet explained. "Someone who acts the exact same way as you." She paused and leaned in. "But they're usually somewhat . . . *evil.*"

"Huh," said Hot Guy. "So am I his evil twin, or is he mine?" he joked, winking at me.

"Oh, you can't be evil," I assured him.

"I can't?" he asked playfully, giving me a wolfish smile. "How do you know?"

I blushed. *Because you're way too cute? Because you're nice to little old ladies?* I wanted to say. "I don't know. It's just . . . a feeling I have," I said in what I hoped was a throaty voice like Devon's. "I mean, this guy here"—I pointed to the cover—"he's just a model, and from what I've read in magazines, *they* can be evil, especially the ones who throw phones at their assistants, but you . . . you're a real person." I started twirling a lock of hair around my finger like Devon did when she was trying to be seductive. The problem was, she had long, thick, raven-black, silky hair, whereas mine was chin-length and on the thin side, which meant that instead of looking sexy all I managed to do was snag it. "Ow," I said as I yanked my finger out, taking a few strands of hair with it.

He handed me the book back. "Be careful, Red—you don't want to lose any of that pretty hair." He gave me another sexy smile. "Is it all right if I call you Red—you know, on account of your hat?"

My mouth fell open. He already had a *nickname* for me! I *knew* our soul-level connection wasn't all in my head.

"Sure," I replied. I quickly shoved the book back into my bag. "So, uh, what's your name?"

"Jack."

"Jack," I sighed. *Jack and Sophie. Sophie and Jack. Mr. and Mrs. Jack* . . . "And what's your last name?"

"Andrews."

I nodded. *Sophie Andrews.* Kind of bland, but it could work. Especially if I hyphenated. *Sophie Greene-Andrews.* Now *that* worked. It sounded so sophisticated!

Jack reached into his knapsack and took out a copy of *Motocross Action* magazine and his iPod. "You want to hear something awesome?" he asked, holding out the earbuds.

"But they already announced that we need to turn off all electronic devices until we're at our cruising altitude."

He smiled at me. "Are you serious?"

I nodded. Of course I was serious. I don't think it was a federal offense if an airline attendant caught you, but I bet they *really* yelled at you. Also, wasn't it a safety thing?

As he leaned toward me, his brown eyes flashing, he opened my palm and wrapped them around the earbuds. "You only go around once, Red."

"According to the Buddhists you don't," I said nervously.

He laughed. "Ha. Not only are you a cutie, but you're funny too!" He pushed my hat up and looked deeply into my eyes. "C'mon, break a rule or two. Live a little."

It was like he was hypnotizing me. I felt like I was going to throw up, but instead of feeling gross or scary it was . . .

the *good* kind of throwing-up feeling. Which, until that moment, I hadn't known existed.

"But . . . I read you can get ear infections sharing these," I blurted.

He laughed. "Well, good thing I cleaned my ears just this morning then." He gave me a smile. "C'mon, take a walk on the wild side."

When he said that, something in me just clicked. Maybe it was the Benadryl, or maybe that reminded me of a song that my parents used to sing on the rare occasions that they had a few glasses of wine and were being silly, but it was like this powerful force invaded my body. As I shoved the earbuds in my ears, he pushed play, and the pulse of drums filled my head.

"Ow," I yelled.

He turned down the volume.

The drums were joined by the wail of a guitar, and I started to bob my head. I usually only like Top 40 dance music, but this sounded amazing. And the skeez factor of sharing earwaxy earbuds wasn't even bothering me. "What is this?" I yelled.

He put his finger to his lips.

Those lips. They were so . . . *puffy*-looking. Like super-expensive down-feather pillows. "Oh. Sorry," I yelled again.

He smiled as he took one of the buds out. "It's Neil Young," he replied.

As he placed the bud back in my ear, I tipped my head down in case the flight attendant walked by. The problem was, the music was so good that it just took me over, and before I knew it, I was tapping my head against the back of my headrest with my eyes closed.

As a guitar solo filled my ears, I realized I had never felt so free in my entire life. I was a rule-breaker. Sure, it was important to not break the *really* important rules—like, say, the need to wait twenty minutes after eating to swim, because that could result in drowning—but if a plane was still on the ground, was it all that bad to have an electronic device on?

A finger poked me on the shoulder, and I opened my eyes to see a very angry flight attendant staring me down.

Okay, so maybe it was.

I took out the earbuds, but the music continued to pour through them.

"As stated over the loudspeaker, all electronic devices need to be turned off until we reach our cruising altitude and the captain announces they can be turned on again," she snapped.

"Oh. I'm sorry," I replied with the most innocent smile I could muster. "I must have missed that part." Omigod—I had just lied to an airline official. What was next? Walking around the cabin when the seat belt sign was on?

"It's my fault, ma'am," Jack said. "I was so busy talkin'

her ear off that we weren't paying attention like we should have. I take full responsibility." Was it my imagination, or did he suddenly sound a whole lot more Southern? He took the iPod out of my hands and shoved it in his pocket. "It won't happen again. I promise." With the innocent look on his face, he could've been Mr. April in the Boy Scouts of America calendar.

"It better not," she snapped.

How could I *not* fall madly in love with someone who was willing to stand up for me like that? Michael never would have done that for me. I wondered then if Michael had texted me yet, but in light of what had just happened, I figured turning on my iPhone to check wasn't such a smart idea.

The minute the flight attendant marched away, Jack turned to me and gave me another lopsided smile. "Look at you, Red. Gettin' us into trouble before the plane has even left the ground," he drawled.

"Sorry," I giggled. I felt a little woozy, but I was pretty sure it wasn't from the Benadryl.

"Flight attendants, prepare for takeoff," the captain's voice said over the loudspeaker.

I leaned my head back against the headrest and closed my eyes as my hat flopped down over them.

The plane had already been in the sky for about ten minutes when I looked down at my hands and realized that I wasn't even holding on to the armrests.

six

Mom says communication is the most important part of a relationship, so I was relieved to discover during the flight that Jack was *really* into talking. In fact, it was almost hard to get a word in. As Harriet snored away and we made our way through the Ziplock bags of cut fruit and trail mix that Mom had made me bring ("Don't waste any of the emergency travel money on those overpriced snacks at the airport," she'd warned), I learned all about Jack and his exciting life.

His childhood was like something out of a movie. He was born in Texas, and when he was three, his parents got divorced and he and his mom went to go live in Arkansas with his grandparents. They weren't dirt-poor or any-thing, like the Mardi Gras float maker who put the spell on Devon's heart in *Validated by Voodoo*, but his mom was never around because she was always out dating so that Jack wouldn't grow up without a father. In fact, she ended up getting married four times.

"Oh, Jack—I'm so sorry," I gasped.

He shrugged. "As my grandma always says, you gotta play the cards you're dealt, even if all you get is a measly two of a kind." So many people in his situation would have turned to a life of crime or something, but there wasn't a trace of bitterness in Jack's voice. As I listened to him go on and on about his childhood, I felt like I did when my history teacher, Mr. Costello, read us an excerpt from Barack Obama's book *The Audacity of Hope*—it was that inspiring.

After graduating from high school ("I'll be straight with you, Red—my As were more in 'having fun' than in math"), he moved out to L.A. to pursue his dream of becoming a rock star. He started a band with some guys he found on Craigslist, and they called themselves Slouching Towards New Orleans. His bass player, who had gone to Yale but dropped out after freshman year, once read a poem with the line "slouching towards Bethlehem" in it and had always thought it would be a cool name for a band, but Jack was worried it was too Bible-sounding and people would think they were a Christian rock group. Because his mom and fourth stepdad weren't happy about his career choice—they had hoped he'd go to the University of Arkansas to study accounting, even though his dyslexia made him really bad with numbers—they cut him off. Which is why, in order to pay the rent, he was currently working as a delivery guy for a Chinese restaurant.

Not only was he ambitious, but it was obvious he was a hard worker and would do anything to support his dream.

"You know where Rock 'n' Roll Ralphs is on Sunset? I live right across the street from there," he said as he threw back a handful of trail mix.

Not wanting to be, as my dad sometimes said about my mom, a total control freak, I stopped myself from suggesting that instead of putting himself at risk for choking, he should eat it the way *I* did: a nut first, followed by a piece of dried fruit, followed by a nut, followed by some fruit, chewing each piece thoroughly for better digestion.

He flicked away the lock of jet-black hair that kept flopping into his eye. I couldn't stop a sigh from escaping. Something about that drove me insane with desire *and* longing.

I thought about it a second. "Near Doheny?" I asked.

"No. In *Hollywood*—at Poinsettia."

"Ohhh . . . right," I replied.

He looked at me in disbelief. "Red. Tell me you've been south of Ventura and over the hill."

"Of course I have," I said. Ventura Boulevard served as the dividing line between the San Fernando Valley and L.A. proper, and the "hill" was Laurel Canyon, which connected the Valley to hipster Hollywood. "I've been wanting to spend more time in Hollywood—it's just been hard to find people to go with." Hollywood was all about tattoo parlors and guitar stores, and the Valley was all about

Pinkberrys and malls. I may have been a Valley girl in real time, but I was a Hollywood girl at heart.

"Well, when we're back in L.A. I'm gonna have to take you on a tour of Hollywood on my new motorcycle."

Oh. My. *God*. He had a *motorcycle*! I knew there was a reason we had bonded so fast. I could just see us now—flying around the sharp corners of the Pacific Coast Highway as we made our way up to Big Sur for a romantic weekend getaway, my arms wrapped tightly around him in his leather jacket, the wind whipping through my hair. I couldn't believe he was already planning things for us to do in the future—that meant he didn't have problems with commitment!

"If you do that, I hope you both wear helmets," Harriet piped up, now awake.

"Oh yes, ma'am," said Jack, sitting up straight again. "Ever since my drummer's girlfriend's cousin slammed into a tree on his brand-new Kawasaki and suffered brain damage and became a paraplegic, I never ride without one." So the wind *wouldn't* whip through my hair. Even though Jack had a tattoo on his forearm of two snakes kissing, that didn't mean he wasn't responsible. I know that with Michael, "responsible" was one of the things that bored me, but with Jack it was a real turn-on.

Harriet nodded approvingly before going back to reading *I Hate You—Don't Leave Me: Understanding the Borderline Personality*.

He turned to me. "That's why I'm going to Florida—to pick up a 1970 Triumph T 120 R Bonneville 650 I scored on eBay."

"Is that a motorcycle?" I asked.

"Not just *a* motorcycle, Red," he replied. "It's like the deluxe supremo version of a motorcycle."

A wave of relief came over me. From the moment I met him I was afraid the reason for his trip was to go see a girl. I was so glad I was wrong.

"Got it for a steal too," he added. It might take my parents a while to get past the tattoo and the lack of a college degree, but they'd love that he was budget-conscious.

Jack pushed the button on his armrest and reclined back. "I think I'm gonna try and take a little nap. I didn't get to sleep until four last night."

I didn't want to think of what he had been doing. Hopefully, it didn't involve kissing a groupie.

"You wanna listen to my iPod while I sleep?" he asked.

"Really?" I asked.

"Sure," he said, cueing it up. "Here, listen to *Everybody Knows This Is Nowhere*. It's Neil's greatest album of all time, if you ask me."

"Diamond?" I asked.

"Huh?"

"Neil Diamond?" I couldn't believe *he* liked Neil Diamond too! Even though he had been popular in the seventies, my parents liked him a lot and I thought he was great.

He laughed as he gave me a little noogie on my forehead. Usually, when Jeremy did that, I hated it, but when it was a love tap like this, it felt really good—sort of like a massage. "No. Neil *Young*, Red. You know, who you were listening to a minute ago."

"Oh," I said, blushing.

"'Cinnamon Girl' is on it. You like that song?"

"Um . . ." I thought about lying and saying yes, but one lie would turn into two would turn into three, and before I knew it I'd be leading a total double life like the Portuguese pet store owner who had told Devon he was a diamond merchant in *Crazed with Craving*. "I don't think I've ever heard it before."

He nodded with approval. "That's what I love about you, Red—you're a straight shooter."

Omigod, he just said he *loved* me. Okay, well, not exactly. But still, he was obviously on his way to doing so.

"Now, some girls—they'd pretend to know it, just to seem cool and all, but you—you're okay with not knowing a lot about classic rock and liking Neil Diamond instead." He cocked his head and looked at me. "Is cinnamon red or brown?"

"I think it's a reddish brown," I replied.

"'Cause I was gonna say—Cinnamon Girl would be another great nickname for you."

"Cinnamon Girl," I said, smiling. "I like that."

He smiled. "Then that's that. From now on, you're Cinnamon Girl. Or Red. You know, depending on the mood."

I tried to contain my excitement. "Okay." Three years with Michael and we never got to the nickname stage, but Jack already had *two* pet names for me!

He handed me the iPod. "Here you go, Cinnamon Girl," he said with a wink before he closed his eyes.

Within a minute he was fast asleep. Quietly, I reached into my purse for my own earbuds and switched them with his. You could never be too careful with ear infections—I didn't want to go deaf and miss all the sweet nothings Jack was going to whisper in my ear as we took walks on the beach at sunset on our honeymoon. Not to mention the fact that although I did it earlier, sharing earbuds *was* kind of gross. As I cracked open *Propelled by Passion,* before I knew it I was no longer on a plane on my way to Florida, but in front of a crackling fire on a cold Montana night as Devon and Dante rekindled their love. As I read, my mouth fell open.

"I know you didn't hear from me once over the last three years," Dante told her, "but it's not like we were broken up or anything—I just pushed the pause button."

I couldn't believe it! Was that in the "Lines to Use on Girls" section of the guidebook that was given to all boys in the hospital when they were born? I had to admit, though, coming from Dante, it didn't sound so bad—especially since he went on to tell Devon that even while he was dating lots of actresses and restaurant hostesses while he was living out in L.A. (consulting on a major Hollywood blockbuster movie where the lead actor played a rancher), *she* was the one he was thinking about as he kissed them. And it's not like Devon was sitting at home in her multi-million-dollar New York City penthouse apartment pining away for him. There had been five books and seven other men during that time, but she had never been able to get over Dante. In fact, the reason those seven relationships had ended (other than the one where that man had to go into the witness protection program) was because Devon *kept telling* the guys how she couldn't get over Dante. Obviously, she hadn't read any of those "Top 10 Things to *Not* Say to a Guy" magazine articles, because if she had, she'd know that talking about how you're still madly in love with an ex-boyfriend is number one on the list.

As Dante threw Devon over his shoulder and hauled her into the bedroom, Jack's head flopped against my shoulder. I waited for him to shift again, but he didn't and his head remained *thisclose* to my cheek, which was beyond thrilling. Except for the fact that I could tell from the way that my cheek started to itch that he used gel in his hair and, because of my sensitive skin, I'd probably start breaking out any minute. I loved that he too had felt the instant bond between us and that—even in sleep—he felt comfortable enough to be close to me. With Michael, it took six months before he'd hold my hand, aside from when we were making out in a dark room, and almost a *year* before he would hold my hand in public.

I glanced at my iPhone peeking out of my bag. *Would* the plane crash if I turned it on to sneak a quick peek and see if Michael had e-mailed me? The sight of the flight attendants making their way down the aisle with the beverage cart jarred me back to my senses.

After I whispered to the flight attendant that I'd like a Diet Coke, she pointed to Jack. "And your boyfriend? Would he like a beverage?"

When I opened my mouth to speak, nothing came out. *Boyfriend?* It was as if a virus had infected the hard drive of my brain and wiped out all the words. I just couldn't believe a complete stranger thought *I* looked like the kind of girl that *Jack* would have as a girlfriend!

"Yes, ma'am, I'd like a Coke, please," I heard Jack's voice say in my ear. "Whaddya say, Red?" he whispered as she poured it. "You wanna be my girlfriend for a while?"

This time I couldn't even open my mouth. A slide show immediately began on the movie screen in my brain of all the amazing girlfriend/boyfriend adventures we'd have together—riding together in the tour bus with his band, jogging together on the beach outside our Hawaiian vacation house. Granted, I didn't actually *like* jogging, but I bet with him it would be fun.

"But I bet someone as cute as you already has a boy-friend," he continued whispering as she put the Coke down on his tray. "Am I right?"

I swallowed. "Actually—"

He put his hand on my arm and grinned. "You know what? Don't tell me. I don't know if I could handle four hours with a broken heart."

My face wasn't just red anymore; now I was *sweating* as well, as if I had just run the six-hundred-yard dash. Maybe jogging wasn't a good idea. I wondered if he had a *Things to Say to Make Any Girl Fall for You* book hidden inside that *Motocross Action* magazine.

I cleared my throat. "So, uh, do you have a girlfriend?" I mumbled.

The right corner of his mouth lifted and his dimple appeared. "Me? Nah. I'm not really the boyfriend type."

My face fell.

"At least not until now, that is," he added with a wink.

Forget needing fuel to fly the plane—*I* could've flown it with the excitement that whooshed from the bottom of my feet up to the top of my head.

"Hey, Red, you don't have anything more to eat by any chance, do you?" he asked. "All I had for breakfast was a slice of leftover pizza."

"I think I have some grapes," I said. See, he *needed* a girlfriend—to make sure he ate on a regular basis.

As I reached down into my carry-on to get them, the plane jerked to the right.

"Omigod!" I yelped, grabbing onto the armrests as my Diet Coke fell into my lap.

Then the plane dipped to the left.

"Oh my heavens!" said Harriet as Lord Byron began to yowl.

Then it dropped a few inches.

"Holy sh—" Jack started to say, before Harriet shot him a look. "—oot," he finished.

With the next swerve, Jack grabbed at my arm and hid his head near my chest. I loved that he already felt so comfortable around me that he didn't feel like he had to act super-brave all the time.

After the plane was upright, he lifted his head. "Sorry," he said sheepishly. "I'm not a great flyer."

"Omigod—me, neither!" I gasped. *Another* thing we had in common.

"Attention passengers," the captain's shaky voice said over the loudspeaker. "Remain calm. I repeat—*REMAIN CALM*. We're just experiencing a bit of turbulence."

"Well, isn't *that* the understatement of the millennium!" snapped Harriet.

The plane rolled and dipped. By this time, plastic cups were rolling up and down the aisle while people screamed. I wondered how long before the oxygen masks fell from the ceiling.

The plane took a nosedive.

"Jack?!" I yelled above everyone's screams, as I clutched on to the armrests for the little life it looked like I had left.

"Yeah?!" he yelled back.

"I just want you to know, I did have a boyfriend," I shouted, my voice vibrating with panic, "but I don't any-more. . . . I mean, *technically*, I still do, but two nights ago he decided we should take a break . . . so we're still together, but it's on hold at the moment," I babbled, reaching for the airsickness bag. "And the reason I'm bringing this up is"—the plane dipped again and my stomach did a roundoff back handspring—"because . . . well, because I want you to know that I would very much like to be your girlfriend. I mean, I know we just met and all, but, yes, I would like to be your girlfriend."

He looked confused. And terrified.

Lord Byron yowled from under the seats.

"Remember when you asked me if I wanted to be your girlfriend?" I yelled, my voice quavering. It felt important to get this settled before we crashed to our death. "Before the plane started to freak out? Anyway, the answer is yes, even though it won't be for long because we're probably going to die any minute."

"Oh. Well, um, thanks," he replied nervously, as the plane shimmied and shuddered back and forth as if it was in belly dancing class. "Thanks a lot. That's really sweet of you. And, uh, I would've been interested in being your boyfriend too."

And then, as quickly as the crazy turbulence had started, it stopped. Within a second, the plane righted itself, and I didn't have to worry about dying anymore. Not physically, at least. But of total and complete embarrassment, yes, because I had just told a totally hot guy I had just met that I wanted to be his girlfriend.

And now I had to sit next to him for the next four hours.

As I wrapped my arms around myself and hid under my hat, I almost wished the plane *had* gone down.

The good news about having a brother with Asperger's is that, when I want to, I know how to be hyper-focused too. Like then, when I chose to be hyper-focused on Devon and Dante and how their passion was propelling them to spend a lot of time kissing. I figured if I looked like I was really busy reading, I wouldn't have to talk to Jack. Like ever again.

All I wanted was to get to Florida and get off the plane—no, *run* off the plane toward baggage claim and Grandma Roz and her "gentleman friend" Art, dive into his red Cadillac that smelled like it had been dunked in pine air freshener, and get as far away from Jack as possible. He had obviously been kidding when he had made that comment about me being his girlfriend. It was just something to say, like, "So do you like Coke or Pepsi?"

"Hey, Red," I heard Jack say quietly a moment later. I was so entranced with how Dante's strong hands were encircling Devon's tiny waist that I almost didn't hear, but unfortunately, his voice had been singed into my soul, like the voice of the Swiss mountain climber, Hans, on Devon's in *Awakened by Ardor*. I would've been able to hear it anywhere, even if he had been speaking at a decibel level that only dogs could pick up.

"Cinnamon Girl," he said.

I turned to him slowly, glad that I hadn't had a chance to get my bangs cut before my trip so that now they were hanging in my eyes. Every little bit of protection against melting from his hotness helped.

"Yeah?" I mumbled.

He held out his hand, which held three smooshed Starburst candies. "You want one? They're a little warm 'cause they've been in my back pocket, but they should be all right," he said with a smile that could've melted the biggest glacier in the world and been responsible for tons more global warming.

I felt like I was being soaked with a cold bucket of relief. Obviously, the way I professed my love (or at least the fact that I wanted to be his girlfriend) back when I thought we were going to die hadn't scared him off, and we were still together! Not only that, but I couldn't believe how thoughtful he was. When Michael offered me candy, it was stuff like Now and Laters that could break your teeth.

I reached for a red one. It *was* warm. "I think I'm going to save it for dessert," I said. Or, you know, the Sophie-n-Jack scrapbook I planned to make as soon as I got home.

He chuckled. "Ohhh . . . I get it. You're one of those girls who waits until *after* the meal to have her dessert."

"Not all the time," I replied defensively. "Once, when my parents were on vacation, I had a cupcake *before* dinner."

He gave me another smile. But this one was more . . . wolfish. "It's kind of fun to mix it up a bit sometimes, huh Red?"

I nodded.

"Wanna try it?"

"Try what?" I asked.

He pointed to the candy. "Mixing it up a bit."

Even though I got the sense that he wasn't just talking about the dessert-first thing, I unwrapped the candy and popped it into my mouth. Because of the heat it was soft and chewy, and the flavor seemed even more intense.

"How is it?" he asked.

"Mffgud." That was I-have-candy-stuck-in-my-molars speak for, "It's good."

He nodded and sat back in his seat. "It's a trip to be wild sometimes, isn't it?"

I nodded again. Being around Jack not only took my breath away; it took my vocabulary away too.

He unwrapped the lemon and the orange ones and popped them into his mouth at the same time. "You see, Red?" he said, leaning in to straighten my hat. "There's a whole other world out there. Stick with me and I'll show it to you."

Boy, was he right.

seven

Although the flight crew kept insisting that what had happened was just run-of-the-mill turbulence, a half hour later the captain got on the loudspeaker to tell us we'd be making an unscheduled landing at Raleigh-Durham International Airport and switching planes. "By no means is this an emergency landing," he announced, "but there's a *slight* malfunction with the fuel tank." The passengers started buzzing. "Seriously, folks, it's absolutely nothing to worry about," he added. My dad freaked if I ever let the fuel in his Volvo get lower than a quarter of a tank ("You'll ruin the engine!"), so I could only imagine what could be happening with our plane.

"You can bet that this airline is going to be receiving a letter from *me*," harrumphed Harriet as we started our descent.

"Aw, it's not so bad. Look at it as an adventure," said Jack, eating a Fig Newton that she had given him. After our

near-death experience, Jack had done a great job of calm-
ing Harriet down, not to mention Lord Byron. Not only did
he have a real way with people, but with animals too.

She patted his cheek. "It's so refreshing to see a young
person with such a positive outlook on life. Are you on
antidepressants, dear?"

He shook his head. "Nope. Just one hundred milli-
grams of living in the moment," he said proudly.

I smiled. Even if it didn't really make sense, it sounded
catchy. Maybe if the music stuff took a while to take off, he
could get a job in advertising. As Dad said, it was important for artists to have a "B" job.

"Plus, Raleigh's real cool. You ever been there, Red?"

I took my tongue out of my molar. "Uh uh," I said, shaking my head.

"Well, I have. My band played a gig there, and afterward we kicked back at this awesome Denny's. It was *huge*.
With a Dennyland playground and everything."

"Wow. That sounds . . . great," I replied. I had only been
to Denny's once, with Michael after a movie, and when we
sat down in the booth, my hand hit something, and when
I looked down it turned out to be a *pair of dentures* someone had left behind. That had to break a few laws with the
Board of Health. Needless to say, we left without order-
ing and I never went back. Even though I had to admit the
brownie à la mode I saw someone eating as we walked out
looked pretty yummy.

"So what kind of gig did you play there?" I asked. An image of him and his band playing in this huge stadium, with girls throwing their bras up on the stage, popped up on the movie screen of my brain.

"It was my drummer's grandparents' fiftieth anniversary at a Rotary Club," he replied.

Okay, so there probably wasn't any bra-throwing going on. At least he was a working musician. I knew from when Devon fell in love with the Parisian mime in *Seduced by Silence* that making a living as an artist was very hard.

"Maybe I'll write a song about you," he said, tapping me on the nose.

"Really?!" I gasped.

He shrugged. "Sure. Why not?" He thought about it for a moment. "What's a good word that rhymes with Red?"

I could hardly believe it. I was becoming his *muse,* just like Devon had been to the Danish painter she fell in love with in *Steamrolled by Satisfaction*! I had never admitted this to anyone—not even Jordan (*especially* not Jordan)—but becoming someone's muse was my life's ambition. I'd probably have to get a second job, but that was okay. To be adored 24/7 and to be told the person couldn't live without you?

I couldn't think of a better existence.

Once we landed and it was safe to turn on my iPhone, I discovered that Michael *still* hadn't e-mailed me. Not even a reply to my "I can't believe you haven't e-mailed me" e-mail. Well, it was a good thing I had Jack. After we deboarded, we walked toward the arrivals/departures board. "They said they're putting us on Flight 18," I said. I looked up at the flights. "Which doesn't leave for . . . *four more hours*?!" That meant that instead of getting in at six o'clock at night eastern time, we'd now be getting in at ten o'clock, which meant I'd miss the original TV movie based on Lulu's book *Singed by Secrets*.

"Awesome," said Jack. "That means we have time to go downtown and do some sightseeing."

I looked at him like he had just suggested we go run around the tarmac naked. "We can't leave the airport!"

"Why not?"

"Well, because you have to be *at* the airport two hours before your departure time."

"I'm not a mathlete, but according to that board, we've got four hours," he replied.

"Yeah, but what if there's a seven-car pileup on the highway on our way back and we get stuck in it while we're waiting for them to remove the dead bodies?" I said. "Or if we're at a restaurant and a gunman comes in and takes everyone hostage?"

I really don't know why he gave me such a weird look. It could happen—both of those things had happened to Devon in the *same* book, *Controlled by Chaos*.

"You know, I never thought about that," he said. "I

guess it's good to think things through sometimes." He smiled. "I have a feeling you're going to be a real good influence on me, Red."

I smiled back. Just wait until I taught him how to use a PalmPilot so he could become super-organized.

Most people probably wouldn't find the American Airlines terminal of the Raleigh-Durham International Airport all that glamorous, but that's because they'd be stuck having to hang out at places like Cinnabon or the Great American Bagel Bakery. I, on the other hand, had Jack to take me to the A-list hot spots.

"Wow, you're a *member*?" I asked as we stood in front of a door that said "American Airlines Admirals Club." I knew from Dad that part of the reason the Admirals Club was so exclusive was because it cost something like five hundred dollars a year to be a member. Maybe Jack was lying when he said that every month he had to struggle to make ends meet and pay his rent. Maybe, like Marco in *Nailed by Nirvana*, he had a huge trust fund and was just *pretending* to be poor until he made sure I loved him for himself and not his money!

"Not exactly," he replied with a wink.

"But it says 'members only,'" I said, pointing at the door.

"Yeah, but I talk my way into these places all the time. It's easy." He pushed the door open. "C'mon."

I paused. Sharing earbuds was one thing, but this?

He grabbed my hand. "Don't worry, it's not like we're going to get arrested."

The minute he grabbed my hand, all my fear about possibly breaking the law by trespassing disappeared. His hand was a little calloused (because of the guitar playing, no doubt), but that didn't stop electric shocks from shooting through my body—like the time my blow-dryer shorted out.

"Good afternoon, ma'am," he said to the woman sitting behind the desk. He leaned in to peer at her name tag. "Ms. Yolanda Crabnick. What a lovely name. Is it okay if I call you Ms. Crabnick?"

From the way she looked us up and down, the "crab" part of her name seemed spot on. "May I see your Admirals Club membership card, please?" she asked.

Jack reached for his wallet, which was attached by a chain to his belt loop, and rifled through it. Not that I was being nosy or anything, but in addition to his driver's license, ATM card, MasterCard, and YMCA card, I spotted *a lot* of scraps of paper with phone numbers written in loopy, girly handwriting.

He looked up at Ms. Crabnick and gave her one of his most charming roguish smiles. "Uh oh. Seems like I forgot it. Think you can let it slide this one time?"

She shook her head. "No card, no admittance," she said firmly.

He sighed. "I *knew* I should have had my secretary double-check my briefcase when I got back from that business trip to Japan. I bet it's in there."

He had such an incredible imagination. If he could come up with great stories like this one on the spot, I could only imagine what a terrific songwriter he was.

But from the way that Ms. Crabnick glared at him, it was clear she didn't buy it.

He smiled at her again. "I'm sure you get this *all* the time, but has anyone ever told you that you could be Angelina Jolie's older sister?"

She rolled her eyes. "As the Admirals Club is a *members-only* establishment, I'm going to have to ask you to leave."

My eye landed on a tote bag next to her chair that said, "Sometimes you have to kiss a lot of frogs before your prince comes along." Peeking out of the top was a book. And I would have recognized that cover anywhere.

"Hey, *Enveloped by Enigmas* is one of my favorites!" I exclaimed. Lulu may have been a fraud, but that didn't mean she wasn't a brilliant writer. I had had no idea that the Balinese masseuse Devon fell in love with in the book was actually a Russian spy who was trying to start a nuclear war.

"You're a Lulu Lavoie fan?" said Ms. Crabnick.

I whipped out my copy of *Propelled by Passion*. "Not only am I a fan," I said, "but Lulu just happens to be my best friend's mother. This is her new book that's coming out next month." I flipped it open. "See—it's even dedicated to me." I left out the part that the dedication was a total lie. And that my name was spelled wrong.

"Oh my," she gasped. "It's like you're famous!" She leaned in. "I really shouldn't be doing this," she whispered, "but why don't you two go on in? Any close personal friend of Lulu Lavoie's is definitely Admirals Club–worthy."

I turned to Jack and flashed him a smile. I was hoping to find him impressed by the fact that I knew a major celebrity, but instead he looked embarrassed that I was the one who got us in and not him. I know I should have been all "equal rights" and stuff, but I thought it was beyond sweet that he wanted to impress me like that. Michael had given up trying to impress me a month after we started going out.

But by the time the doors hissed closed behind us, Jack was back to being his confident self.

As we strode over to the table with the free snacks (okay, maybe not strode, because we were both dragging our carry-ons), I realized I had finally arrived. Maybe at Castle Heights I'd always be invisible (or worse, exceptionally visible—especially since the calendar fiasco), but here at the Raleigh-Durham International Airport, all eyes were on me for all the right reasons. Or maybe it was because I kept bumping into things because my hat was too big. Still, it was nice to get the attention.

"Great view, huh?" asked Jack as he threw some roasted peanuts back and chased them with a swig of his complimentary soda. He really needed to be more careful about potential choking hazards.

"Oh yeah," I agreed, sipping my Diet Coke. This place was so fancy, they even put a slice of lemon in the soda. We were so close to the tarmac that I could actually see one of the baggage handlers smoking a cigarette next to a tank that said, WARNING: FLAMMABLE.

"It's like having third-row center seats at a Neil Young concert," he said.

I had never considered looking out at a runway strip all that interesting before, but with Jack, everything seemed exciting. As I listened to him crunch his ice, I was hit with one of my psychic premonitions. They didn't happen often, and they usually had to do with pop quizzes, but in this case I had the vision of us sitting in Admirals Clubs around the world while Jack toured with his band. Instead of places like Raleigh and West Palm Beach, we'd be in airports in Paris and Rome and Tokyo.

My iPhone buzzed, and I almost knocked over my soda. Sure, I was totally focused on Jack, but maybe there was the *teensiest* part of me that was wondering if Michael would finally come to his senses and realize how badly he'd screwed up. Not that I was interested in pushing the play button with him again. I looked at the screen. Just an e-mail from Always 16 about an upcoming sale.

Jack pointed to my phone and shook his head. "I gotta

say—I don't get that being-in-constant-communication thing. I mean, sure, I have a cell and all, but I can't get my e-mail on it. Sometimes you just want to be unplugged and enjoy the moment, you know?"

I nodded. He was so . . . *Buddhist.*

"So how long have you been with your boyfriend?" he asked.

The image of Jack and I enjoying a crepe at an outside café in Paris was replaced by Michael's face covered with chicken pox. Talk about a buzzkill. "My boyfriend?" I repeated.

He laughed. "Yeah, your boyfriend. Didn't you say on the plane that you had one?"

Not only was he Buddhist, but he was *psychic.* He must have intuitively known that even though I had no interest in getting back together with Michael, I was still waiting for that e-mail saying he had been an idiot.

I pointed at his soda. "So are you a Coke person or a Pepsi person? Personally, I like Tab best, but it's really hard to find," I blabbered nervously. "I've only found two minimarts in L.A. that carry it, and even then, they don't have it *all* the time. Just, like, every three months or so."

He gave me one of those half-smiles that drove me crazy. "Did you know that you're trying to change the subject and not answer the question?"

"No, I'm not," I replied, fiddling with the salt and pepper shakers.

He took the pepper shaker from me. Of course, he

took the pepper. It was spicy, just like him. "Red, changing the subject is the only thing I get straight As in—especially when it comes to talking about relationships."

"Well, like I said, he's not exactly my boyfriend at the moment. It's kind of on hold."

"Oh man, did he push the pause button or something?"

I nodded, stunned. Was this something that *all* guys did?

"Sorry to hear that," he said. "That's a tough place to be. How long have you guys been together?"

"Three years."

"Three years?!" he hooted. "That's like almost a third of your life!"

"Actually, it's 18.5 percent of it," I said. "What's the longest you've been in a relationship?"

He thought about it. "Three months."

Okay, so he just hadn't met the right girl yet. And it was impressive that rather than stay in something that wasn't working, he wasn't afraid to be alone, which, according to my mom, was the reason most people were in relationships.

"No, wait . . . it was two months," he said.

Okay, so he was a free spirit—until now. Until me.

"But because the pause button's been pushed, technically I'm, you know, *available*," I said. I was, right? I wasn't sure on the etiquette of this situation. I'd need to do some research to find out for sure. I pointed to a row of computers. "How much do you think it costs to use one of those?" I wanted to Google, "If your boyfriend has pushed the pause button, is it okay to kiss someone else?"

"They're free," he replied. "That's one of the perks of hangin' in the Admirals Club."

It really *was* pretty exclusive. I bet they even had free Tampax in the ladies room.

We moved over to the computers and sat down. It wasn't like I was *trying* to look at Jack's computer, but because there was a fat guy who smelled like cabbage at the computer next to me, I found myself leaning toward Jack, and my eyes just *happened* to glance up at his screen after he logged on to his mailbox. And they *happened* to see that he had thirty-three new messages.

"Wow. Have you not checked your e-mail in a few days?" I asked, pointing at the screen.

"No. I checked it before I left this morning," he replied, clicking on a message that I saw was signed, **Lots of luv, Brandi xoxoxoxoxoxoxoxoxoxo**. I tried to read it, but only got through **Hey Jack, How r u doin?** before he closed it and opened one signed, **Miss u TONS, Brianna xoxoxoxoxoxoxoxoxoxoxoxo**.

"So is it, like, lots of . . . junk mail . . . or something?" I asked, with one eye on my screen and the other on his.

"No. Just e-mails from friends and stuff."

Yeah, "friends" that all happened to be *girls* it seemed, as I snuck another glance at his screen in time to see one signed, **Mwah! Kylie xoxoxoxoxoxoxoxoxoxoxoxo**.

Jack wasn't technically my boyfriend yet, but just knowing that all these girls with names that ended in vowels had his e-mail address made me feel like I was going to explode. Some people might call the way I was feeling "insane with jealousy," but I liked to think it just meant I was really passionate. That's the explanation that Devon gave whenever she started doing things that were a little on the obsessive side, like spending hours doing Internet drive-bys on her boyfriends or using *67 to block her number and call whatever guy she was in love with that month just to hear him say, "Hello? Hello? Hello?!"

I had never felt jealous when I was with Michael. Not once. Maybe that was part of the problem. Maybe if I felt about Michael the way I felt about Jack at that moment—with my heart beating like I had had four Red Bulls in five minutes—things would have worked out and I'd be sitting in the waiting area of the gate reading my book instead of sneaking into a members-only lounge with Jack.

I willed myself to stick to my own screen and focus on my Googling, which, unfortunately, didn't help, as most of what came up were articles about DVD players.

"I think I'm done," I said, as I caught sight of the **See ya soon, Kristi xoxoxoxoxoxoxo** on his screen.

"Okay," he said. "Let's go get some lunch." He looked over at me. "Are you reading my e-mails?" he demanded.

I could feel the color leave my face. "I . . . no . . . I just," I stammered.

He punched me on the arm. "I'm just joshin' with you," he said, giving me one of his lopsided smiles that were as addictive as York Peppermint Patties.

We started to gather our stuff.

"But I gotta say—you're even more cute when you're freaked out, Red," Jack said. "Makes me want to—I don't know—*protect* you."

I knew it was so antifeminist, and Jordan would've broken up with me as a friend if she ever heard me admit it, but when Jack said that, I felt this whoosh of warm energy go through my body.

I wondered if he said things like that to the vowel girls. My name ended in a vowel too, but that was different. I was a vowel girl who really *wasn't* a vowel girl. But as we made our way to the gate, he reached for my hand, and I stopped wondering.

There was only so much a girl could focus on when a hot guy was holding her hand and scrambling her brain.

You'd think a person would go insane with boredom having to spend four hours in an airport, but because I was with Jack, the hours felt like *minutes*. After the Admirals Club, he took me to Pizza Hut Express for lunch (okay, technically, I took him because he had forgotten to go to the ATM that morning and the one in the airport was all the way down at the other end of the terminal), to TCBY for dessert (again, I paid), and to Starbucks for Frappuccinos (ditto). He even bought me a Raleigh magnet at the gift shop (yes, me again) so I would have a souvenir of our time together.

The only real blip was the conversation we had as we ate our second dessert at Cinnabon. "Jack?" I asked, as I tore off a piece of my sticky bun.

"Yeah?" he said, as he polished off his.

Was it my imagination, or did he keep staring at the blonde girl with the I'M NO ANGEL T-shirt two tables down from us. "Can I ask you something?"

"Sure," he said.

"You know all those e-mails you had in your inbox? Are all those girls really just friends, or are they, you know . . . *friends*?" I rearranged my chair to block his view of her and adjusted my hat.

He sat back in his chair and swiped at the lock of hair that kept flopping over his left eye. "Okay, I'm gonna be straight with you, Red," he sighed. "Not all of them are just friends. Some are a little . . . *more* than friends."

I nodded, hoping I looked a lot stronger than I felt.

He slumped down in his chair. "I don't know what it is about you, Red. Even though we just met, I feel like I can tell you this and you're not going to think I'm a horrible person. It's like I know you'll accept me no matter what."

If that wasn't the definition of soul mates, I didn't know what was. But was this the part where he was going to tell me that he had recently escaped from prison, like Manuel,

116

the Chilean revolutionary who Devon fell in love with in *Tortured by Tumult*?

"Here's the thing," he continued. "I'm like a stray dog. As long as the door stays open, I'm always going to come back. But the minute it starts to close?" A sad look came over his face as he shook his head. "I start to freak. And I bolt." He raked his hand through his hair and shot a quick glance at the blonde. "I've been doing a lot of work on it in therapy, but my shrink says when a pattern's been ingrained so deep, it doesn't change overnight."

I gasped. Forget the stray dog part. "Omigod—you're in *therapy*? That's so great!"

If he was in therapy, that meant he could *change*! He could stop being a stray dog and turn into one of those super-loyal dogs that never left your side, because they were so grateful you had rescued them from being put to sleep!

The blonde got up to leave and winked at Jack as she walked by. I swore he winked back.

"Jack, are you flirting with her?" I asked. He couldn't have been, right?

"What?! Of course not. She just looks a lot like my cousin Luanne who passed away from leukemia a few years ago." He sighed. "They say time heals, but not a day goes by that I don't think about her."

I melted. He was so loyal—and Luanne was just his *cousin*. He was so in touch with his emotions. I could only imagine how horrible he'd feel if his soul mate died.

He slumped down in his chair again. "You're lucky, being able to stay in a relationship for a long time like you did." He sighed. "You're so . . . *normal*. But me?" He sighed. "I don't know . . . once those fireworks stop popping I'm outta there. It's a problem."

I sat back in my chair and pushed my hat up.

He had no idea how alike we really were.

The flight to West Palm Beach was turbulence- and drama-free. At least on the outside. All the drama was in my head, with my worrying about how to tell Michael to forget the pause button (I wanted to push the stop button) and trying to figure out what I was going to wear when Jack and I "hung out" the next night. ("'Date' is such a . . . four-letter word, Red," Jack had said.)

But after we landed and Jack and I made our way out into the baggage claim area, my stomach started twisting into knots like a balloon animal. Next to going to the doctor, Grandma Roz's favorite hobby was pointing out people's faults. I highly doubted she would be able to see Jack's true essence, underneath his longish hair and pizza-stained black T-shirt. Not the way I did. By the time I saw her standing next to the luggage carousel in a purple velour tracksuit that made her look like a giant grape, I was so nervous I thought I was going to throw up.

Was I going to have to choose between my soul mate

and my family like Devon did in *Anguished by Amour* when her churchgoing parents threatened to disown her after she started living with the Hollywood movie director before his divorce was final?

I gazed at Jack as he stopped to switch his carry-on to his other shoulder, and I realized that if it came down to that . . . well, I was in too deep to *not* choose him. I fiddled nervously with my Chunnels. I only hoped it didn't get too ugly and that at least Jeremy would still talk to me.

Grandma Roz squinted at the two of us as we got closer. "Sophie? Is that you?" she yelled.

"Uh huh."

"What are you wearing those ridiculous sunglasses for inside?" she demanded once we were in front of her. "They're so dark you're going to trip and break your neck!" She pointed to my cowboy hat. "And that *meshuga* hat? You think you're going to a dude ranch?"

"Hi, Grandma," I sighed. "It's nice to see you." I held my breath as I leaned in to hug her. Ever since I could remember she had smelled like a combination of Lysol and sardines.

After she let me go, she looked around. "Where are the candelabras?" she asked, panicked.

"Dad boxed them up and I checked them."

"You checked them! The family heirlooms?!" She clutched at her chest. "Oy, my heart. I know your father doesn't think I was a good mother, but does he hate me so

119

much he wants to *kill* me?" Her eyes narrowed. "At least tell me he used Bubble Wrap and peanuts."

"He did."

"And where's the lox and whitefish?" she demanded.

I pointed to my carry-on. "In here."

"Ahhh . . . so *that's* what I was smelling!" Jack said.

I was so busy being terrified of my grandmother that I almost forgot Jack was there. She turned toward him. "Who are you?"

"Grandma, this is my friend Jack," I said in my best granddaughter voice. I figured "friend" would go over a lot better than "soul mate." "We met on the plane," I added.

She grabbed his arm and yanked it toward her face for a better look. "Is that a tattoo?" she demanded.

"Ah, yes, ma'am," he replied nervously. I hadn't seen Jack flustered before. Seeing another layer of him made me like him even more.

She turned to me. "He must not be Jewish," she sniffed, "because if he were, he'd know that he can't be buried in a Jewish cemetery now."

I was so mortified I wanted to climb on the luggage carousel and disappear around the corner.

"No, ma'am—I'm not Jewish," Jack admitted. "I was raised Episcopalian, but I have always very much admired those of the Jewish faith because of their strength of character and everything they've been forced to endure and overcome in history." I couldn't stop my mouth from falling open. It was like someone had implanted a book report chip in Jack's brain.

Grandma Roz nodded. "You're darn right," she agreed. Her eyes narrowed again. "You have an accent. Where are you from?"

"Pointed Fork, Arkansas, ma'am," he said proudly.

"Arkansas? Not a lot of good delicatessens there, I bet."

Jack chuckled. "No, ma'am. There's not." He turned to me. "Sophie, you told me all about how smart and beautiful your grandmother was, but you forgot to mention she was funny too."

No wonder he was able to get so many girls' phone numbers.

Grandma Roz snorted. "Get out of town."

"Believe me, I may not have been an A-plus student in school," he said, "but one subject I sure aced was being able to spot and appreciate a gorgeous woman."

Grandma Roz turned so red she was almost as purple as her outfit. "Well, back in the day maybe I turned some heads, but now I'm an old woman who's about to die any minute."

"Old?!" hooted Jack. "I swear, as we were walking up, if Sophie hadn't told me you were her grandmother, I would've thought you were her *mother*."

For the first time in my sixteen years on the planet, the I-have-a-lemon-stuck-in-my-mouth look left Grandma

Roz's face. It would be pushing it to say she was pretty at that moment, but at least she resembled one of those nice, sweet grandmothers I had read about in fairy tales, like in "Little Red Riding Hood" or something—the kind whose idea of quality time with her only granddaughter would be shopping at Loehmann's or baking cookies rather than forcing her to read the numbers on the digital blood pressure cuff and look at brochures of burial plots.

She slapped him lightly on the arm. "Oh, stop joshing," she snorted.

Jack rubbed his arm. "No, I'm *serious*," he said.

She stared at him for a second before the *teensiest* hint of a smile crossed her face. It was so subtle that most people would say she looked as grumpy and annoyed as always, but because I had spent my life waiting for it to appear, there was no way I would have missed it.

If there had been any doubt that Jack cared for me, this attempt to win my family over sealed the deal. It was like when the carpenter who was really an heir to a mining fortune built Devon's half-sister new shelving units for her double-wide trailer in *Engulfed by Exaltation*.

A loud honk signaling the arrival of the luggage sounded. "Come on, let's hustle," said Grandma Roz. "I don't want anyone trying to steal those candelabras."

She was only five foot two, but Grandma Roz bulldozed through the crowd like she was a ginormous football player. "So Jack, why are you in Florida?" she demanded once we got near the carousel and were waiting for the box to come out. The smile was gone, and she was back to resembling a detective on a TV show.

"I'm here to pick up a motorcycle I bought on eBay, ma'am. A 1970 Triumph T 120 R Bonneville 650."

Her eyes narrowed. "Two- or four-cylinder engine?"

"Two," he replied, surprised.

She nodded approvingly. "Makes for a much smoother ride."

Jack and I looked at each other. "Um, Grandma? How do you know about motorcycle engines?" I asked.

She sighed and her eyes glazed over. "It was 1976. Your grandfather had decided he wanted a little break—"

I gasped in recognition. "He pushed the pause button on your relationship?"

She nodded. "He sure did. And I ended up taking your father to Paris for the summer. I think he was twelve at the time."

"You've been to Paris?" I said. Up until that moment I didn't think she had ever been anywhere other than Scarsdale, New York—where she raised my dad—and Delray Beach.

She nodded. "Italy too." A faraway look came over her face and she sighed again. "His name was Jean-Pierre."

"Whose name was Jean-Pierre?" I asked.

She rolled her eyes and turned back into the grandmother I knew and feared. "The man who took me on the bike," she replied slowly, as if I was in remedial reading. But that dazed look returned to her face. "We zipped around the streets of Paris, with my arms wrapped tightly around his waist—"

"Okay, we get the picture," I said. Obviously, I wanted to hear the story, but this was getting uncomfortable.

"The wind blowing through my long blonde hair—" she continued.

"Your hair was blonde?" I said. Ever since I could remember, Grandma Roz's hair had resembled a gray Brillo Pad.

She shot me a look. "I wasn't always an old lady, you know," she said.

"I bet you were a real looker back then, ma'am," said Jack. "Not that you're not *still* one."

She turned to me. "He's very nice, this Jack. You always did have good taste in friends, Sophie. Except for that girl with the boy's name—the one who dresses like she's a soldier."

"Jordan," I replied. "But getting back to Jean-Pierre— what happened?" I asked impatiently. I couldn't believe my grandmother had what Lulu always called a "torrid past." It was just like in *Decimated by Devotion* when Devon found a trunk full of faded tabloid articles in her parents' attic about an "unidentified, raven-headed vixen seen canoodling" with a "very married" box office star and figured out the raven-headed vixen was *her own mother.*

"Enough about Jean-Pierre. That was a long time ago," she said.

A big cardboard box came sliding down the chute. The words on its side read, FRAGILE!!!! FAMILY HEIRLOOMS INSIDE!!!!! EXTREMELY VALUABLE WITH GREAT SENTIMENTAL VALUE!!!!

"There it is!" Grandma Roz yelled. As a giant suitcase followed and slammed into it, she clutched at her chest. "Oy, I don't know if my heart can take this," she moaned.

"Don't worry. I'll take care of it," Jack said as he pushed his way toward the front. Unfortunately, every time he lunged for the box, he missed it, which is why we had to wait for it to come around again.

"Here you go," he said a few minutes later, out of breath, as he placed the box carefully at Grandma Roz's feet.

She whipped out a Swiss Army knife and in an instant cut through the layers of packing tape Dad had slapped on there. As Styrofoam peanuts flew up in the air, she lifted out one of the candelabras and examined it. With its eight arms it looked like a very skinny octopus. "Oy, thank God it's all right." She clutched her heart again. "The relief could kill me." She turned to Jack. "Oh, Jack, how can I thank you?" she asked.

He shrugged. "All I did was grab the box."

"Yes, but who knows the damage that could've been done if you hadn't gotten it when you did." She patted his cheek and turned to me. "He's a good boy, this Jack." She turned back to him and gave what was probably the first sweet smile I had ever seen on her face. "So where are you staying while you're here, Jack?"

His stomach rumbled. "Whoops—sorry about that. Guess I'm a little hungry."

Before the "-gry" had even made its way out of his mouth, Grandma had her pleather designer knockoff bag open and was shoving ziplock bags full of Goldfish, dates, and Fiber One cereal at him. "Of course you're hungry—all that heavy lifting! Here, eat! Eat! It's the least I can do to thank you!"

I knew that Jack had won her over completely. While most grandmothers are always shoving food at people, Grandma Roz held on to her snacks as if a giant earthquake was going to arrive any second and wipe out all the grocery stores. The last time I was at her house I had caught her counting the cookies in the pantry and writing down the figure on a notepad.

"Aw, you're sweet, but I couldn't take your snacks, ma'am."

He couldn't? He had taken all of mine on the plane.

"Of course you can!" she boomed. "And enough of this 'ma'am' *mishegas*—it's Roz to you!" I had never seen her take to anyone like this. Not even family. *Especially* not family.

"Thanks, Roz," he replied. With a shrug, he took all three bags and started tearing into them. "Trip came about so quick I didn't have enough time to look into a motel room or anything," he said, munching on some Fiber One. "I'm sure I'll find something." He sighed. "I just hope it's not too expensive, because I'm really trying to watch my pennies. Save up for a new amp."

"Motel *schmotel*," scoffed Grandma Roz. "It's highway robbery the prices they charge here. You can stay at Art's. He's my gentleman friend."

"Aw, I couldn't do that," he replied.

"Of course you can. I hate to see young people throwing away their hard-earned money, especially in this economy."

She did?

"Well, maybe just for tonight," he finally said.

She clapped her hands. "Now come on, kids—we need to hustle. Art's probably *schvitzing* to death because he refuses to turn on the air conditioner. He says it wastes gas."

Jack wasn't an A student, but he was smart enough to know you didn't argue with Grandma Roz.

I don't know if you'd call what was between Grandma Roz and Art *love*, but they were soul mates in that they were a perfect match: she talked nonstop—mostly complaining—while he kept quiet, grunting just enough to let her know he wasn't completely ignoring her.

They had met at the finals of the Twenty-second

Annual Garden of Eden Bingo Tournament two years after Grandpa Max had passed away, and as Grandma Roz liked to say, it was "comfort at first sight." In addition to having the same kind of shaggy rug-like toupee as Grandpa Max, Art also wore a Windbreaker and Docksider shoes and Polo cologne. "Comfort at first sight" doesn't exactly sound romantic, but I guess when you're old, it's the smarter way to go so you don't have a heart attack from the passion.

Art kept his own place—which just happened to be next door—so that Grandma Roz wouldn't look like what Devon's mother called a "hussy," having a man who wasn't her husband spend the night. But every time I had been in Florida, I heard him in the bathroom at five o'clock in the morning clearing his throat so loudly it sounded like he was hacking up a lung. If that didn't give it away, his booming, "Well, *bubelah*, looks like we fooled 'em again" as he left to go back to his own place did.

Even when Grandma Roz wasn't around, Art wasn't a big talker. In fact, as we sailed to the Garden of Eden in Art's red Cadillac at thirty-five miles an hour, other than "Hi, Sophie" and "Nice to meet you, Jack," all he did was add a few "Of course you're right, Roz's" to the conversation. But, as Grandma Roz liked to say, there was a lid for every pot—no matter how banged up and tarnished and scratched—and he had replaced Grandpa Max as hers.

After making him spend ten minutes arranging the candelabras on the mantle in the living room ("Art, what are you, blind? I said move the one on the left *half* an inch—that was *three-quarters* of an inch!") we went over to his condo so Jack could see his room.

"Wow, this is *great*," Jack said as he checked out his reflection in the smoked mirror above the dresser. Decorated in black and mauve, the room looked like a floor display of one of those cheesy furniture stores that always had a huge GOING OUT OF BUSINESS! banner in front.

Jack turned to Art. "Thanks, Mr. Weinstein. I really appreciate the opportunity to bunk down here."

Art gave a nod and a grunt as he walked over to the shelf that held his autographed baseball collection and started dusting them with the handkerchief he kept in the pocket of his high-waisted jeans.

Jack turned to my grandmother. "Roz, I can't thank you enough for letting me stay here. You're a real saint. Wait—do the Jews have saints?"

She patted his cheek. "You're welcome, Jackie. You think I'd let you stay in a motel where there's bedbugs?" She looked at her watch. "Okay, kids—it's already ten thirty. Sophie, say good night."

"But it's only seven thirty L.A. time," I pleaded. "I'm wide-awake."

"No back talk, young lady."

"Actually, Grandma Roz, I was wondering if it would be okay for Sophie and me to take a walk around the complex," Jack said. "Get a little fresh air to fight off the jet lag."

She smiled and ruffled his hair. "That's a wonderful idea, Jack. You've got a good head on your shoulders." She reached into her purse and took out a small aerosol can. "But you have to promise me you kids will be very, very careful and keep this pepper spray with you at all times. There's been a series of break-ins around the complex over the last few weeks."

Jack took it from her. "Don't you worry—your girl's safe with me," he announced, putting his arm around me and giving me a wink.

I was so shocked at how much my life had changed in the last few hours, I felt like someone had sprayed pepper spray on *me*.

The billboard on the side of the highway with a picture of a couple dressed in golf clothes billed the Garden of Eden as "Southern Florida's premiere destination for luxury living in the twilight years," but the truth was that the place was as old-looking as its residents, a.k.a. the Edenites. As long as you didn't get too close, it all seemed okay. But if you looked hard you saw that the lounge chairs were frayed, and the tennis nets were ripped, and the shuffleboard court had weeds growing out of the cracks in the concrete.

But that night, as Jack and I walked in the moonlight toward the Pagoda of Delights (it sounded romantic, but it was really just an area with vending machines that sold soda, candy, and first aid supplies), I *did* feel like I was in the Garden of Eden. Or, better yet, one of those super-exclusive islands in the Caribbean where movie stars went for Christmas.

"I just love that it's a full moon tonight," I sighed as Jack shook the vending machine trying to knock a package of Ring Dings free. Every time Devon met one of her soul mates it was a full moon, so I considered it a very important sign. "Isn't it beautiful?"

After giving the machine a few punches, Jack stopped and looked up at the sky. "But it's not a full moon."

I squinted. "It's not?"

He poked at his fist and cringed. "Ow. No, it's more like . . . a half-moon."

I pushed up my hat and squinted again. "Huh. I guess you're right." Oh no—was wearing my Chunnels indoors starting to ruin my eyesight? I'd have to Google it later to see if there were any documented cases of blindness due to wearing sunglasses indoors. "Well, whatever it is, it's pretty," I said, winking at him.

He peered at me. "You okay, Red?" he asked. "You got something in your eye?"

"No, I'm fine," I replied as I took a step closer to him. I couldn't believe how *bold* Jack made me feel. I felt like I was a science beaker, like when someone adds too much hydrochloric acid to it and it starts to smoke.

"Good. Just checking," he said as he went back to

shaking the machine. "Ha! Got it!" he yelled a second later. He grabbed the package out of the bottom and ripped it open with his teeth.

I sighed. If Michael had done that, I would've found it gross, but with Jack, it just showed so much . . . *coordination.*

"Want one?" he asked after shoving a Ring Ding in his mouth.

"Okay," I replied, suddenly starving. He was already thinking of us in terms of sharing everything equally.

Even though my response had come barely a second later, it was too late. Before I had even gotten the word out of my mouth, the other Ring Ding was already in his.

"Oh. Whoops," he said with his mouth full.

"Don't worry about it," I said.

"You sure?"

I nodded. "Let's go sit," I said, pointing at a pair of lounge chairs over near the Jacuzzi.

"You know, you're really cute, Red," Jack said as we sat listening to the Jacuzzi bubble. Because it was broken, the sounds it made were more like little farts than bubbles, but that was okay. If Jack was next to me, a jackhammer would've sounded good.

"I am?" I whispered back, pushing my hat up so I could gaze into his eyes. Right then, my iPhone buzzed, and I whipped it out, trembling. Although I was officially annoyed that Michael hadn't responded yet—to the point where, while Grandma Roz was showing Jack her magnet collection, I had texted him again saying, "Okay, I'm now officially annoyed that you haven't written back"—now was not the time to have him do it. Luckily, it was just an e-mail from Claire's about an upcoming sale.

He leaned in closer. "You gotta learn to turn that thing off," he said, "so it doesn't ruin the moment."

"Sorry," I whispered. I moved to push the power button off, but I just couldn't bring myself to do it. Instead, I just silenced it.

"Anyway, I was gonna tell you—I decided that red cowboy hat kinda girls aren't cute."

My face fell. "They're not?"

"Nope. They're *hot*," he replied with a wolfish grin, and leaned in closer.

This was it. This was the moment that I would finally get to experience what Devon felt all those times when she was kissed by all those guys from all those different countries in all those books. This was the moment I would know what the real definition of the word "passion" was.

And then, just as our lips were about to touch, the webbing underneath my butt gave way, and I fell straight through the chair onto the ground. Luckily, my hat kept my head from smacking on the concrete, so I didn't get amnesia, like Devon did in *Muddled by Memories*.

"You okay?" he said as he helped me up.

I patted myself to make sure nothing was broken.

My body was okay, but my soul was rattled. Everything happened for a reason. And I knew that even though my relationship with Michael was technically paused, this was clearly a sign from the Universe that until everything with Michael was settled, it was uncool to kiss another guy.

eight

I knew Jack had totally and completely won Grandma Roz over when she told him to take as much lox and whitefish as he wanted at breakfast the next morning. But it was what happened after she finished her stewed prunes that made it clear she *really* trusted him.

"Jack, did you get in touch with the motorcycle man?" she asked sweetly as she polished the candelabras for about the tenth time in thirty minutes. It was too bad Jeremy wasn't around.

"I sure did, and unfortunately, 'cause of a family tragedy—turns out his brother's arm was snapped off by a gator—he won't be back in town till the end of the week. So I thought after breakfast I'd start calling around to find a motel."

"Don't be silly. You'll just stay at Art's," Grandma Roz said.

"Thanks, Roz, but I couldn't take advantage of your

kindness like that," he drawled. Was it my imagination, or did Jack seem to really pour on the Southern thing with her?

"To be honest, in light of the break-ins, I feel better knowing there's a strapping young man nearby to protect us. You know, Sophie, there was another robbery last night!"

"There was?" I said.

She nodded. "Yes. Myrna Gladstein, over in the Winds of Change building. The robber took her silver menorah, if you can believe that." She pointed at Art, who was busy reading the racing form. "Art was taking his nightly walk at the time, but he didn't hear a thing."

"That's because I had already taken my hearing aid out," Art said without looking up from the form.

"Well, if it'll make you feel better, Roz, I'll stay then," Jack said.

I knew it would make *me* feel better.

"So would you kids like to take the Buick and do a little sightseeing?" Grandma Roz said as she started polishing the other candelabra.

My jaw almost hit the floor. Her '82 Buick was her pride and joy. She never let *anyone* drive it—not even my dad, her own son. She was so paranoid about getting a scratch on it that she barely drove it anymore, and when she did, she insisted on parking like a mile away in the most deserted part of a parking lot so there were no cars on either side.

Jack turned to me. "Whaddya say, Red? Want to do some exploring?"

"Sure," I shrugged, still dumbstruck from Grandma's offer.

A few minutes later, red cowboy hat on my head and Chunnel sunglasses on my face, I was humming along (a little off-key) to a singer named Jimi Hendrix on the classic rock station Jack had found as we inched our way down the main drag of Delray Beach behind other Buicks and Cadillacs. The music helped keep my mind off of Jack's tailgating, but I couldn't help trying to push the imaginary brake on my side of the car. As the song ended and morphed into something called "Stairway to Heaven"—which, according to Jack was a classic slow-dancing song back in Arkansas—I rolled down the window to get some fresh air. Right then, I understood more than ever what it meant to be alive. Forget the Urban Dictionary definition of Sophie Greene. The *real* definition was a girl who didn't have a care in the world because she was out on the open road sitting next to her soul mate.

"Red?" Jack said as we turned off the highway a few minutes later.

His voice sounded far away, due to the fact that I was busy trying to recall what life had been like before I knew him. It had only been a day, but I felt like Jack had been in my life forever. That was probably because that's how it is with soul mates.

I turned toward him. "Huh?"

He chuckled as he reached over and punched me in the arm. "That's another thing I love about you—you're a real thinker." He winked. "That's really sexy." He tapped his head. "Most girls I seem to hang with . . . there's not a lot going on up there, you know? But you—you're real different. I bet you kicked ass on your SATs."

I blushed. He appreciated me for my mind and not just for my body. Not that I had much of a body to appreciate, but still.

We stopped at a light, and Jack turned back to me. "I was saying, you know what else we did to this song?"

I shook my head.

"We would make out."

"You would?"

"Uh huh," he said, unlatching his seat belt and moving toward me. "Like big time."

"You . . . your seat belt," I sputtered.

"Don't worry. I'll make sure to put it back on when we start moving again."

"So . . . you'd make out during the dance?" I said nervously. "But didn't the chaperones get mad?"

He started to scoot closer. "Uh huh."

"Would you get in trouble?" I whispered.

He leaned in even closer. "Yup."

I knew some people would accuse me of being too much of a romantic, but years from now, when my daughter asked me where I was when her father kissed me for the first time, I didn't want to have to say it was in a Buick with fast-food restaurants all around. I wanted to wait until we were in a nicer setting. Plus, there was the whole on-hold-with-Michael and Universe-not-yet-approving situation.

"Hey look!" I said nervously. "There's a Denny's! Want to stop for lunch?"

He shrugged, and shifted back into his seat. "Okay."

My only other experience at Denny's had been gross, but with Jack, I saw the plastic booths and bad overhead lighting with entirely different eyes. When Devon was on vacation she usually had lunch on private yachts or cute little cafés overlooking the valleys of France, but Denny's was romantic in its own way. Well, it would have been if we hadn't been seated behind a family with six-year-old twin boys who thought it was hysterical to throw onion rings at someone's head. In this case, *my* head.

"Ow," I winced as another one caught me in the back of the neck. The crispy ones could really scrape your skin.

"I think it means they like you," Jack said as he crammed half a pancake into his mouth. "Like when a boy pulls your hair." He leaned over and pushed my bangs out of my eyes with his sticky hands. "I bet *lots* of boys used to pull your hair on the playground."

I practically melted into the sticky plastic booth. I'm sorry, but Michael had never said romantic things like that to me. His idea of romantic was, "No, those jeans don't make your butt look fat."

A person would have to be a nun or a peace corps volunteer in Africa to not be affected by Jack. The connection I felt with him as we sat there eating our food—tuna melt for me, Grand Slam with extra sausage for him—was beyond powerful. We just had so much in common: both of our mothers were born in June, we both liked *The Simpsons*, we both liked creamy peanut butter rather than crunchy. I gazed at him while he ate half of my sandwich, and I felt understood in a way that I never had before. It was like I didn't have to explain myself to him—it was like he had climbed inside my brain and just . . . *got* me.

After we had finished, the waitress put the check on the table.

"Thanks"—Jack grinned and leaned in to read her name tag—"Kimber," he said. I wasn't sure, but it seemed to me that he was leaning in way too close, but maybe he was nearsighted.

She rolled her eyes and walked away.

"So should we go?" I asked.

"Sure," he said, standing up and stretching. As he did, his black T-shirt rode up (even though it looked identical to yesterday's, I knew it was different because there wasn't a pizza stain on it), and I could see his belly. Instead of being the smooth, rock-hard six-pack that Lulu described Dante as having, Jack's was a little . . . squishier. With a couple of moles. That was okay, though. I actually didn't want to be with a guy who was too perfect. It would be like being with a Ken doll. Moles made a person a lot more interesting. "Let's go get ourselves into some trouble," he said as he started to walk toward the door.

"Wait. What about—"

He stopped and turned. "What about what?"

I pointed to the table. "—the check?"

He smacked his forehead. "Darn it! I forgot to stop at the ATM again!"

I wasn't one of those girls who expected a guy to pay all the time, but this was getting a little annoying. "Didn't I see a credit card in your wallet, though, when we were at the Admirals Club?" I asked. "We could, you know, split it."

"Yeah, but I hate to use a card unless it's a real emergency. I don't know if you've been following the news, but credit card debt is a huge problem in our country at the moment. Think you can cover it, Red? I'll pay you back as soon as we hit a bank." He gave me one of his smiles. "I promise."

I reached for my emergency envelope of cash. I didn't think that lunch at Denny's was an emergency, either, but what choice did I have? It wasn't like I was a dine-'n'-ditch girl. "Okay," I sighed. At this rate I'd be lucky if I had enough money left to buy any sunblock.

He reached for my hand. "Thanks, Red. Now let's go get into some trouble."

I didn't know if I was going to get in trouble with Jack, but if I hung out with him much longer, I was in danger of going broke.

Letting a guy who's not officially your boyfriend (because you haven't officially broken up with your other boyfriend) push you on a swing in the playground next to Denny's might not be considered trouble. But when he stops pushing and holds the swing still and gets *thisclose* and stares into your eyes and says, in an Arkansan drawl, "I hadn't noticed how pretty your brown eyes are until now. Maybe I should call you 'Brown-Eyed Girl' instead of 'Cinnamon Girl'?" it feels like it could turn into trouble.

"Thanks," I said. "Except . . . they're green."

He squinted. "They are?"

I nodded.

He squinted some more. "Are you sure?"

"Pretty sure," I replied. He might have been color-blind, but it was the thought that counted.

Instead of the half-smile, he leaned in closer, almost like he was about to kiss me. "Well, whatever color they are, they sure are gorgeous."

He was so close I could smell the onions from his lunch on his breath. Except that he hadn't had onions. But the way he looked at me when we were *thisclose* I almost didn't care.

A playground with cars whizzing by wasn't that much more romantic a spot than a Buick for a first kiss, but I was finding it hard to control myself. I closed my eyes, ready to be rocketed into the fourth dimension.

"Hey, look over there!" he said. "A thrift store! I *love* thrift stores!"

I opened my eyes. "You do?" I said. I had never actually been in one before. But I'd seen something on the news about how a couple's apartment had become infested with bedbugs because of a couch they had bought at one, and that had totally grossed me out.

"Yeah. They always have lots of cool stuff." He grabbed my hand and pulled me off the swing. "Come on, Red— let's go check it out."

"Okay," I sighed, and followed him. I guess I had just gotten yet another sign from the universe that it still wasn't time.

It was amazing what people thought they could get money for: old vacuum cleaners, five-foot-tall brass statues of Native American chiefs, typewriters. Even an oil painting of the White House done on black velvet.

"Hey, check this out," Jack yelled, holding up a rusty sword and pretending to fence. I smiled—he looked like an action-adventure star.

The old guy behind the counter who had been watching us like he was just waiting for us to steal something took the toothpick he was chewing out of his mouth. "You break it, you buy it," he snapped.

Jack glanced over at him and reluctantly put the sword back. "I'm just lookin', dude. *Sheesh.*"

"Hey, maybe we should get going," I said nervously, afraid the guy might take one of the guns out of the case in front and shoot Jack for having an attitude. "We're missing prime laying-out time." Also, I still needed to pick up some sunblock.

"Red, it's Florida—it's *always* laying-out time," he replied as he walked over to the shoe department of the store. "Holy cow!" I heard him exclaim.

I looked up from a bunch of Barbies that were missing various body parts. I could understand buying a doll that was missing one arm, especially if it was a good deal, but one that was missing her arms *and* her legs? "What is it?" I asked.

"Close your eyes, close your eyes—I just found the perfect gift for you! When'd you say your birthday was?"

"I didn't, but it's January 21st," I said, closing my eyes.

"Oh, what the heck—it'll just be an early birthday gift then."

More talk about the *future*! We really were perfect for each other.

"Are your eyes closed?" he asked.

I nodded.

"Okay, you can open them."

When I did, the smile of anticipation on my face melted into confusion.

"Those are . . . motorcycle boots," I said.

He nodded. "Aren't they awesome?"

"Well, yeah, but they're . . . used." Not only was the black leather scuffed to the point where it didn't even look black in some places, but on the bottom of the sole, someone had written, "I love Bruno," inside a big heart.

"It *is* a secondhand store, Red. Plus, you want 'em broken in—believe me." He shoved them toward me. "Here, try them on."

"Yeah, but that means they've been on someone else's *feet*," I said. Sharing earbuds with my soul mate was one thing, but who knew how many athletes' feet or plantar warts had been inside these boots?

"We got Peds if you want 'em," said the guy behind the counter.

The look on Jack's face was so hopeful I couldn't say no. "Okay," I shrugged.

As Jack held one of the boots out and I slipped my Ped-covered foot inside, it was hard not to feel like Cinderella—especially because to my surprise, the boots were a perfect fit. Well, they would be after I put a pair of extra-thick wool socks on.

He stood up and looked at me. "Wow, you look *hot* in those."

I clomped over to the floor-length mirror. Jack was

right—between the boots and my hat, I *did* look hot. Who knew that in addition to being a red cowboy hat kinda girl, I was also a motorcycle boot one? Plus, if you ignored the big scratch down the side of the right boot, they looked exactly like the pair of Prada ones that the Norwegian Pulitzer Prize–winning playwright had bought Devon with some of his prize money in *Dazzled by Despair*.

"Now you'll be all set for when I take you for that ride," he said.

More future talk! It was like whenever he did that, I couldn't help but throw caution to the wind and stop being so . . . *good*. I threw my arms around him. "Oh Jack—I love them!" I couldn't believe he was so thoughtful. The only presents Michael gave me were gift certificates to places like Pinkberry and the Gap.

"Good, I'm glad." He turned to the guy. "How much?"

"Twenty bucks."

"Twenty bucks?!" Jack hooted. "But they're all beat up!"

The guy shrugged. "Okay. I'll take ten."

"That's better," he said with a nod. He started to reach for his wallet and then stopped. "You probably just take cash, huh?" he asked the guy.

The guy pointed to the big sign on top of the counter that said, WE ACCEPT VISA, MASTERCARD, AMERICAN EXPRESS, AND DISCOVER . . . FOR A SMALL FEE.

"Small fee, huh?" He turned to me. "Whaddya say, Red? You want to add this on to my tab? It's only ten bucks. But don't worry—I won't forget to pay you back for them. Otherwise, it wouldn't be a gift."

My grin melted, and I sighed and took out the envelope.

"Holy moly, is that what I think it is?!" Jack exclaimed, pointing into the distance.

The guy looked up. "What? The Bozo the Clown bop bag?" he asked, motioning to one of those inflatable toys with sand on the bottom that popped right back up whenever you punched it.

"No. Next to it," Jack said, pointing to a motorcycle that was covered with dust. "Is that a 1974 Kawasaki 400 S 3 Mach II?"

"Yep," the guy replied nonchalantly, taking out one of the guns from the glass case in back of him and starting to polish it.

Jack walked over to it and started using the bottom of his T-shirt to clean the dust off. "This is a *classic*," he announced. He looked up at the guy. "Does it run?"

"Of course it runs," the guy snapped. "This is a legitimate business. You think I'd sell stuff that's broken?"

I looked over at the obviously broken vacuum cleaner and the toaster oven that was missing the door, but decided pointing that out to a guy holding a gun probably wasn't a smart idea.

Jack turned to me and gave me one of his crooked smiles. "Hey, Red—wanna break in those boots?"

147

I looked down at them. They already *were* broken in. "You mean go for a ride?"

He nodded.

Seeing that my life had become one nonstop adventure in the last twenty-four hours, it seemed stupid to put a stop to it now. "Okay," I shrugged.

"Gotta leave a deposit of fifty bucks," the guy said.

Jack turned to me. "You got it?" He must have recognized my look. "Don't worry, we'll get it back when we bring the bike back."

We'll get it back? Even though I liked being a couple with him, I didn't know if it was a good or a bad thing that Jack was talking about *my* money like it was *ours*.

He turned to the guy. "Where are the helmets?"

The guy picked two up from the floor behind him and plopped them onto the counter.

"I can't wear my cowboy hat?" I said, disappointed. Plus, the idea of putting yet another thing on my body that was used sort of grossed me out. What if its previous owner had lice?

"Red, that would be very irresponsible. Safety always comes first," Jack scolded, picking up the smaller of the two helmets. "Don't worry. When we get back to L.A., I'll buy you your own."

I took it from him and plopped it on my head.

"But I gotta say—you're wilder than I thought you were," he said with a wink.

I guess I was. I was even starting to surprise myself.

* * * * * * *

The minute we got out on the open road I understood why all those years I knew I loved riding on the back of motorcycles even though I hadn't actually been on one before. The wind, the feeling of being so connected to nature . . . it was just so . . . *freeing*. Well, as freeing as it could be riding around the parking lot. The thrift store guy wouldn't let us leave the property. And maybe my hair wasn't actually *moving* because of the helmet, but still, it was an adventure. I hadn't realized until I wrapped my hands around Jack's waist how freedom was something I craved—just like peanut butter Twix bars dipped in butterscotch sauce when I was PMSing. I also hadn't realized until then that Jack had what my mom called "love handles" on the sides of his waist. His black T-shirt hid them, but like the moles, they just made him more human and real. It was good to know that instead of being perfect, he was a regular human being.

As we drove around in circles in the parking lot at five miles an hour (any time Jack tried to go faster, the engine stalled), I tilted my face up to the overcast sky and realized I felt just like Devon when Antonio, the Italian waiter (who was really a sculptor), took her for a ride on his Vespa through the streets of Rome in *Exalted by Eros*. Yes, we were driving by garbage cans and an old, rusted lawnmower instead of centuries-old buildings and gelato stands, but still, it was romantic.

"Hwyadog?" Jack yelled out as we made yet another lap.

"What?!" The high-pitched drone of the engine made it hard to hear. When Devon rode on the back of a motorcycle, the engine "purred." With this one, it was more like it "whined."

"I said, hwyadog?!" he yelled, louder this time.

"What?!" I yelled back again, even louder.

He stopped the motorcycle, turned around and took off his helmet. Even though his hair was standing up like he had just put his finger in a light socket, it still looked good. "I said, hwyadog?"

"What?" I said again.

He took my helmet off. "I *said*, how are you doing?"

Now that we were stopped, the whole thing wasn't so romantic anymore. The parking lot looked . . . like a parking lot. And instead of the sexy samba music that seemed to be playing whenever Devon was with a guy, I had the sound of the traffic whizzing by on the highway. "Oh. I'm fine," I replied. "Well, actually, I'm a little nauseous, to be honest. I think some of those fries at lunch weren't cooked all the way through. Do you think we could go home now?"

He moved a piece of hair out of my eye. "Whatever you want, Princess."

Princess. Michael had called me that once. But only once, so it wasn't an official nickname, but still, it reminded me again of that connection we had once had. Suddenly, I was flooded with guilt.

"I just want you to be happy," Jack said, touching my arm.

"That's sweet," I replied, moving back a little. I had been ready to kiss him back at the playground, but now, thinking about Michael, I wasn't so sure.

"Hey, do you think we can stop at that Stop-N-Slurp across the street before we go back so I can get a snack?" I said nervously. "I'm feeling like my blood sugar is falling. That never happened until I got mono last year. Have you ever had mono?" I babbled.

"Nope. Never have," he said, getting so close I could see that he had a nose hair peeking out of his nostril.

"You're lucky. It's really awful. I had to stay in bed for a month and then—"

"Red?"

"Yeah?"

"Are you going to shut up so I can finally kiss you, or do you just wanna keep talking about stuff like mono and measles and chicken pox?"

At the words "chicken pox," I leaned back so far I almost fell off the bike. "Chicken pox" equaled "Michael" equaled "my boyfriend." Another sign. The Universe really *really* did not want me doing this. I just wanted this whole Michael thing to get settled already so I could check the guilt and move on with my life.

I whipped out my iPhone. **I need an answer, Michael!!!!!!** I typed.

151

When we got back to the condo, Grandma Roz was sitting at the kitchen table polishing the candelabras *again*. "I've got a surprise for you kids," she said.

"What is it?" I said warily. I felt like I had had more surprises in the last four days than I had in my entire sixteen years and three months on the planet.

"Well, first off, I thought Jack might like to taste my brisket." She turned to him. "The women in my mah-jongg league say it's the best they've ever had," she boasted. "I've been slaving away in the kitchen over it all afternoon." She patted Jack's cheek. "Not that I mind."

Sheesh. As far as I knew she only made brisket for the Jewish holidays, and every time, she complained about how time-consuming it was.

"We'll dine by candlelight with the candelabras," she went on. I couldn't believe it—no one had ever actually *used* them as far as I knew. "*And,* as we eat the macaroons I got for dessert, I thought Jack might want to see the video from your Bat Mitzvah, Sophie."

"What?! Noooo!" I cried. As far as I was concerned, looks-wise, my Bat Mitzvah was the darkest day of my life. I had begged Mom to let me get a body wave a week before, and it had gone seriously wrong, and the trapeze dress I had worn made me look like the poster child for *How to Commit Fashion Suicide.*

"That sounds awesome, Roz," Jack said, ignoring my freak-out. "There aren't any Jewish people in Pointed

152

Fork, so I've always been curious about what a Bar or Bat Mitzvah was like."

All through dinner I felt nauseous. Not just because the brisket was undercooked, or because the heat from the sixteen blazing candles was giving me a headache. It was more because I was nervous about whether Jack would still like me when he saw the red cowboy hat–less version of me.

Once dinner was done, and we moved into the living room, I started getting even more nervous. Then Grandma started up the video. The macaroons were chocolate-covered, so they made things a little more bearable, but still, if they gave out Olympic medals for sitting still while dying a slow death from embarrassment, I would've won the gold. Why hadn't anyone *told* me I had been so off-key as I warbled the opening prayers that day? It was beyond humiliating to have to listen to my thirteen-year-old self, especially because I was sitting next to a working musician. Thankfully, the plastic on the couch helped to keep me in my seat. It was on all the furniture—including the La-Z-Boy recliner—and the green carpeting was also covered with plastic runners. Mom was always saying that next thing you knew, there'd be velvet ropes blocking the room off, like they have in museums.

What was amazing was Jack's reaction to the whole thing. Instead of snickering or yawning, he seemed to be genuinely interested.

"Wow, Red—that's real impressive, the way you know

153

all that Hebrew," he announced after the part where I read my Haftorah.

"Don't take this the wrong way, but I never would've thought you had so much rhythm," he said as thirteen-year-old-me did the Electric Slide.

"I *knew* you had a bit of a wild side!" he said during the part where I sat in the chair while the adults hoisted me over their heads and marched me around the dance floor.

Was he serious? I couldn't help looking around to see if there was a hidden camera somewhere.

"Thanks for pretending to be interested in the video," I said later as we walked toward the Pagoda of Delights.

"What do you mean, 'pretend'?"

I stopped. "Well, you didn't actually *mean* all that stuff you said . . . did you?"

"Of course I did."

I searched his face for one of his half-smiles or a wink, but he looked serious.

"But—"

"But what?" he said.

I double-checked the lounge chair to make sure it wasn't in danger of breaking, and flopped down on it. That girl in the video didn't have a wild side. That girl wasn't who I wanted to be—she wasn't who I wanted him to think I was. But I didn't think I could hide it anymore. "We're from such different *worlds*." Devon was always from a different world from the men she fell for, but this was a whole new thing for me.

He shrugged. "Arkansas is part of the United States."

Even though it was still at least seventy-five degrees out, I wrapped my arms around myself. Maybe if I could scrunch up into a small enough ball, I could disappear. "Yeah, I know." I sighed. "But you're probably used to going out with girls like Juliet DeStefano. Even if her first name ends in a consonant," I muttered to myself.

"Who's Juliet DeStefano?" he asked, confused.

"This girl at my school. She's exciting and mysterious and"—the time had come to be completely honest with him—"well, I'm . . . *not*," I said quietly. "Sure, being with you has brought out a different side of me. Like, for instance, before I met you, I never would've put on boots that had been on someone else's feet. But, Jack, I feel like you need to know this: I'm really pretty ordinary."

He sat down next to me. "Ordinary?! What are you talking about? You're not ordinary at all! You're smart and funny and sweet. And with the hat and the boots?" He whistled. "Well, no disrespect or anything, but you're a scorcher, Red."

I smiled. "Thanks, Jack, that's sweet of you, but seriously—I'm just . . . normal. I like to go see romantic comedies at big multiplex theaters, and I watch reality television, and I take vitamins. Oh, and I start to freak out if I go more than two days without eight hours of sleep a night."

He shrugged. "I like to sleep too. Sometimes I don't get up till one in the afternoon."

I gave one of my heavier sighs. "I'm just afraid you'd get bored of me." I went on. "I'm not wild or bipolar. I mean, even if I wanted to, I could never be one of those girls who did the push-pull thing with a guy to keep him interested."

"Yeah, you don't seem like the type," he sighed. "That being said, you're an excellent listener, which is a hard quality to find in a person. In fact, you remind me a lot of my shrink. I'm not gonna lie—I don't have a problem meeting girls. But you, Red—you're different." He thought about it. "It's like you've got a lot of weight to you. I don't mean fat or anything like that—more like . . . substance. Those other girls—the Brandis, the Andis, the Randis—they're fun and all, but they're like Chinese food. A little exotic, and spicy, if that's what you want, but a half hour later you're hungry again." He pointed at me. "But you . . . you're more like a hearty stew. Fills you up and keeps you warm."

I smiled. At first listen a "hearty stew" didn't sound very romantic, but the more I thought about it, the more I realized it actually *was*. I was marveling at how it was the sweetest thing anyone had ever said to me, when my iPhone buzzed. But for once in my life, I didn't pick it up and I let it buzz. I was done being a slave to an electronic device. Whatever it was could wait, especially since it was probably just another announcement of some sale. But the buzzing was so . . . *insistent*. Which is why I decided to be a slave just for old time's sake and picked it up.

> **yo. what up? i've been thinking about it & i think we should push the stop button. it's not fair to hold u up while i figure stuff out. peace, M**

It wasn't supposed to happen like *this*. Michael was supposed to call me, and I was going to tell him that *I* wanted to push the stop button! This was the second time that he got to be the one to say things weren't working. It was so not fair.

"Everything okay, Red?" Jack asked.

As I looked at him, all anxious and caring, I realized that, actually, it was better it went down like this. Now, when Michael found out about Jack, he wouldn't be so heartbroken. He'd be able to tell himself that he had broken up with me even though the truth was that I had ended it in my mind way before that.

What mattered now was that since Michael had made the decision and pushed the stop button, all the guilt I felt about wanting to kiss Jack was gone. The Universe finally gave me the go-ahead! Maybe the Pagoda of Delights wasn't the most romantic setting in the world for a first kiss, especially with the ice machine making so much noise, but it sure was better than outside McDonald's, which is where Michael and I had first kissed.

"Everything's fine," I replied with a smile. As Devon also liked to say, I was now "unencumbered by the shackles of duty and gliding toward my destiny." I wasn't exactly sure what that meant, but I had a feeling it perfectly described how I felt. "In fact, it's all good," I added as I leaned in, finally ready to kiss my soul mate for the first time.

Before his lips even came close to touching mine, I started to hear the fireworks and the marching bands and all those other loud noises that Devon heard when a hot guy kissed her.

Then his lips *did* touch mine, the fireworks stopped, and it got super-quiet.

It wasn't like I had a ton of experience—I mean, other than Michael, the only other guy I had kissed was Camp Guy—but I knew enough from movies and books to know that kissing didn't involve gnawing at a person's lip like it was corn on the cob.

After what felt like hours but was really only about thirty seconds, Jack stopped gnawing and came up for air.

"Wow, Red," he said, wiping his mouth. "That was *awesome*. I don't want you to take this the wrong way, but I didn't think you'd be such a good kisser."

How could he even tell how good or bad I was? He was mauling my face, and I had barely even had a chance to kiss back. "Uh, thanks," I replied warily.

He flopped back on his lounge chair and grinned. "We've got great chemistry, huh?" he asked with a wink.

I leaned back on my own lounge chair. I was too dazed to even answer him. How could someone so hot be so *bad* at kissing? And what did this mean for our relationship? Were we doomed? When Dante kissed Devon for the first time, it had gone on for hours, and afterward she compared it to drinking two 2-liter bottles of water after having taken both a spin class *and* a yoga class. I, on the other hand, felt like I had just swallowed a cup of salt, because of the brisket.

He stood up. "Man, that made me thirsty. I'm gonna get a Coke. Want anything?"

I shook my head.

He leaned down and pecked me on the cheek. "I'll be right back."

I nodded. Maybe the kiss had been so bad because he was just really nervous. Even though it was hard to believe, beautiful people did, in fact, get nervous. I had read about it once in a magazine article about a twenty-year-old Russian supermodel.

As I watched him bang at the soda machine, I looked up at the three-quarters-full moon.

"Hi, God?" I said quietly. "I know we don't talk a lot, so You might just ignore this because of that, but if You *are* listening, I just wanted to ask if maybe You could do something about the kissing stuff? You know, like teach Jack how to do it better? Because I was thinking . . . I mean, the fact that You put Jack in that seat next to me on the plane . . . it just *had* to be because You want us to be together and fall in love, right? It's just too . . . *fateful*. Like how Devon walked into the diner in Montana just as Dante was walking out and they bumped into each other and Devon almost fell because she was wearing high heels in the snow and so she grabbed onto Dante's arms to steady herself and he pulled her close and they fell madly in love at that moment."

A light went on in one of the condos near the gazebo, and an old woman in curlers glared at me from the window. I wasn't sure if it was because of Jack's banging or because it looked like I was talking to myself instead of God.

"Anyway," I continued once she put the shade back down, "I know kissing isn't everything, but it *does* mean a lot—especially since, You know, I don't really do . . . more than that."

Boy, even though I wasn't Catholic, it was still really weird talking to God about sex stuff.

"Ha! Gotcha!" Jack yelled as I heard the can clunk down to the bottom of the machine.

"Okay, listen, I have to go because he's coming back," I whispered. "But I'd *reallyreallyreally* appreciate anything You can do. Thanks."

As I waved to Jack, I turned my head to the side. "Oh, right. Amen," I added.

After he chugged down half the can, he yawned. "Wow, I'm beat." He patted his stomach. "Must be that third helping of brisket. Ready to go in?"

"I guess so," I said as I stood up. I knew the emotional and intellectual connection in a relationship was much more important than the physical stuff, but I couldn't help feeling completely bummed out. Did that make me beyond shallow? I hoped not.

"Cool. But I think I need another one of these first," he said, grabbing me by the shoulders and kissing me again.

After he chewed on my face for a few seconds, I pushed him away. God must have been busy listening to someone in the Middle East or Africa or something because this kiss was just as bad. This time he *licked my nose*. Obviously, I couldn't rely on Him to fix this. The time had come to take matters into my own hands.

"Jack?"

"Yeah?"

"I was thinking . . . my mouth is on the small side, so maybe we could try it with a little less . . . tongue?" I said nervously. Was it rude to give guys kissing pointers? I had never had to say anything to Michael, because he was a good kisser, so I wasn't sure.

"You mean like this?" he asked, leaning in and kissing me gently. He pulled away. "How's that?"

It was definitely better. Kind of like a B-minus instead of a D. "That was great. Just one more thing: do you think that instead of tilting your head to the left, you could tilt it to the right instead?"

"I'm left-handed, though," he replied.

I wasn't sure what that had to do with anything.

He smiled. "But I'll give it a try," he said, leaning in.

That was the last thing I remembered before the fire-works started exploding. Just a few at first. But within an hour, he was up to an A-minus. Jack may have been teaching me how to walk on the wild side, but *I* was teaching *him* how to kiss.

nine

It's funny how you can go from hating something to loving it, which is what happened for me with Florida that week. Suddenly, the fact that it took three times as long to get anywhere in the Delray Beach/Boca Raton area than it did in the rest of the world—because old people are horrible drivers—didn't bother me anymore. In fact, I started to see it as cute and charming. The idea that the old man at Red Robin was yelling at the waitress because she had brought him real butter and not light canola oil spread for his baked potato wasn't annoying; instead, I saw that he loved his wife so much he wanted to stay alive and be with her for as long as possible. The fact that it took Jack and I almost fifteen minutes to get from one end of the mall to the other because we were behind an old woman with a walker wasn't frustrating; it just gave us time to gaze into each other's eyes as we enjoyed the cheesy piano player playing "It Had to Be You."

"Red, you're so much fun to make out with," he said

one evening as we came up for air. We had driven to the beach to watch the sunset, but because a huge downpour started when we got there, we were stuck in the Buick. Not that I minded.

"I feel the same way about you," I whispered, reaching down into my boot to pull up my sock.

Occasionally, I still thought about Michael. But even when things were at their best with him, they had never been this good. For the last few months I had spent our make-out sessions—the few that we had had—going over the chemical element tables and conjugating the past perfect tenses of French verbs in my head. But with Jack I was 100 percent right there in the moment. Even when I tried to jump ahead into the future and think about the fights we'd have about the appropriate age for our son to get a motorbike, or whether it was okay for our daughter to get a tramp stamp of a butterfly before she went off to college, something about being with Jack just took me out of my head and slammed me back into my body. He was like a living, breathing yoga class.

"It's weird, but I just feel so *safe* with you," he went on. "Maybe it's because most of the girls I go out with are real drama queens and you're so . . . not."

I smiled. I was so glad I had talked to him about being a normal girl. Ever since he compared me to a hearty stew, I had been okay with not having a dramatic life like Devon or Juliet. Girls who wore seat belts and sunblock could still be sexy.

I used to hate the way that the way-too-bright Florida sun made everything look so harsh—especially the scowls on the faces of all the Edenites whenever kids made the mistake of making noise in the pool as if they were having fun. But the next morning, I sat on a lounge chair slathered in SPF 55 (thankfully, I still had enough of my emergency money left over to buy some) with zinc oxide on my nose and my red cowboy hat on my head, and it looked like the Edenites were charmed and not at all annoyed by Jack's whooping and splashing as he did cannonball after cannonball off the edge of the pool. I mean, I couldn't tell for sure, because I was wearing my Chunnels, but how could they *not* find him as adorable as I did?

"Hey Red, watch this!" he yelled as he climbed out of the pool in the neon yellow swim trunks Grandma Roz had insisted he borrow from Art.

"Okay, I'm watching!" I yelled back, cringing slightly when he almost tripped on an oxygen tank as he made his way back to the edge of the pool.

"You sure you're watching?" he shouted, doing knee bends and cracking his knuckles.

"Yup!" I yelled back. It was very inspiring to be around a person who had such high self-esteem and so much confidence. Not only didn't he mind people looking at him, but he actually seemed to love it.

He walked back a few paces and, with a running start, did a flip into the water.

"Jack, that was *awesome!*" I yelled once he came up for air. I don't think he had planned to land on his belly like that, but the fact that he could stand that amount of pain (the smack of his stomach on the water was *really* loud) was beyond impressive.

He swam over to the side of the pool and jumped out, making his way through the sea of Edenites who stared at him in awe. Although, when I squinted, I realized that maybe they were staring at him in annoyance. He *was* dripping all over them. But one of the things I loved about Jack was the fact that even though the old people didn't even try to hide their disapproval when they first met him and saw his tattoo, he still was able to completely win them over with his charm. Even Grandma Roz's best friend, Mrs. Bernstein (who was crankier than Grandma Roz), was now calling him *bubelah*.

When he got to me, I put aside my copy of *Propelled by Passion* so he wouldn't drip on it and handed him a towel.

He pointed to the book. "Wow, I can't believe what a fast reader you are. So that'll be the third time you've read that?"

I nodded. Now that we had talked and sealed our bond with numerous make-out sessions, I felt comfortable enough to be my truest self with him. Which is why I told him all about Devon over breakfast that morning. I even read some of the more romantic parts of the book aloud to him.

He plopped down on the lounge chair next to me and

reached for his faux Ray-Ban aviator sunglasses. As we lay there with our faces tilted up to the sky—him in his Rye-Buns and me in my Chunnels—I felt like part of an ad for a fancy Caribbean resort. As long as the motorized wheel-chair that belonged to the woman sitting in the chair next to me was cropped out of the photo.

I turned to him and took my glasses off. "Jack?"

"Yeah, Red?" he replied, sliding his own glasses up his face and staring out into the distance. I wasn't sure what he was looking at because all I saw was an overly tan, bikini-clad woman in the distance, but she was at least forty, so I doubted he was looking at her.

"I just wanted to say . . . well, these past few days, being with you has been just great."

"I feel the same way," he replied.

I reached for the sunscreen. "Want me to do your back?"

He shook his head. "Nah, I'm okay."

"I know you like to live on the edge, but you need to take care of yourself more," I said.

"You're right," he said, turning his back to me. "My shrink says a lot of my self-destructive behavior patterns are because I have low self-worth."

"Anyway, as I was saying, not only has it been edu-cational, like learning all about classic rock and stuff," I continued, "but I think the most important thing is you've really taught me how to stay in the moment."

He turned his head toward me and smiled. "I have?"

"Uh huh. I just love that you're all about the 'now' rather than last week, or next month. You're just . . . *here*." I sounded like Luca, the Italian olive oil heir turned yoga teacher that Devon had a mad, passionate rebound affair with in *Excited by Envy* when she was trying to get over Dante.

Once I was done doing his back, he settled into his chair again and reached for the ziplock bag of pistachios Grandma Roz had given him. "Thanks, Red. That's a huge compliment." When I had said I liked pistachios during my last trip, she had complained about how expensive they were, but when *Jack* mentioned in passing that he liked them, she immediately sent Art out to get some. Of course, I was glad that she loved Jack as much as I did, but you'd think because she was *my* grandmother, she'd care more about whether I was better fed. He threw a pistachio in the air and caught it in his mouth. Then he turned and flashed me that brain-scrambling grin.

I smiled back and started tickling his right arm with my now-chipped Cotton Candy nails. Obviously, although I was keeping *some* of my responsible self, in light of my new life with Jack, I would be making the leap to Dark as Midnight at my next manicure. "It's just so cool," I continued, "because when I'm in the moment like this, I'm not thinking about the future, you know?"

"I hear you," he said. "I *never* think about the future," he added proudly.

"I mean, I'm not thinking about what's going to happen with us when we're back in L.A.," I said, "if, you know, this was just a Spring Break fling . . . or if it's going to continue." Okay, maybe I *had* been thinking about it. Just a little bit.

He shifted in his chair.

"And I'm not thinking about the fact that if it *does* continue, what's going to happen to us when I go east for college, and whether our relationship can handle the distance." It felt so good to feel comfortable enough to be able to say exactly what was on my mind without thinking it through.

He shifted again. He was so fidgety. Maybe he had to go to the bathroom.

"Or how we're going to manage to see each other when your music career takes off and you're on the road a lot." I sat up and looked over at him, squinting against the sunlight. "Jack? Are you okay? You look a little pale."

"Uh, yeah," he said, reaching for my water bottle and chugging it down. "Just too much sun, I think."

I settled back in my chair. "Anyway, I just wanted you to know that I'm not thinking about any of that stuff. I'm just enjoying the time we have together, rather than, I don't know, having any sort of *expectations* about what's going to happen with us."

He seemed to relax a little. "That's good, Red. That's good."

"My mom always tells us that expectations are

resentments just waiting to happen," I announced. I went to tickle his arm again.

He pulled it away. I understood. When I wasn't feeling well I didn't like anyone touching me either. "Your mom sounds really smart," he said.

"Yeah, she kind of is," I agreed. "It's the shrink thing." The only dumb thing she had said was that love at first sight didn't exist and that you had to know someone for at least three months before you really knew who they were.

I settled back in my chair and pulled my Chunnels back down.

Who knew life could be so good?

And who knew it could get so bad so quickly?

The next afternoon, after Jack and I worked on darkening our tans (or, in my case, worked on turning my SPF 55–protected skin from white to pink), we hung out in Grandma Roz's living room watching *Mystery Falls*, her favorite soap opera that she TiVo'd every day, while she and Art "rested their eyes" over at Art's place.

"The acting is pretty good on this show," Jack announced as he chomped away on the TV tray full of snacks that Grandma Roz had prepared for him. I couldn't believe how, after a lifetime of rationing out potato chips, she was now throwing around bags of cookies and microwave popcorn like they were free samples that had just arrived in the mail.

"And who's that guy again?" I asked, shifting on the plastic-covered couch to unstick my legs.

"That's Reynaldo," Jack replied, as the guy began to play tonsil hockey with a blonde dressed in a sexy nightgown even though it was the middle of the day. "Your grandma told me that before he was Reynaldo, he was Diego, Savannah's ex-husband. He was in a bad car accident and had to have major facial reconstructive surgery, so now Savannah doesn't recognize him anymore. She thinks he's the cable guy."

Over the last few days, Jack had gotten hooked on soap operas faster than I had gotten addicted to Lulu's books.

"The same thing happened to Devon in *Titillated by Trouble*, but she thought he was one of those guys collecting donations to end global warming."

"Huh. Your iPhone's buzzing," Jack said.

"It is?" Over the last few days with Jack, I had stopped being so attached to it. I didn't check it every five seconds for texts. I did still e-mail Jordan and Ali at the end of the day to give them updates, but otherwise I just left it in my bag.

"Aren't you going to see who it's from?"

"No. It can wait," I said.

He pointed to the TV. "But the buzz is making it hard for me to concentrate on the show."

"Oh. Sorry," I said, picking it up.

I clicked on my new e-mail message, and my face paled.

Dear Sophie,

It turns out that there's not a lot to do when you're stuck at home waiting for your scabs to fall off other than think and stuff, which is what I've been doing over the last few days.

I know I pushed the stop button on our relationship, but after a lot more thought, I'd like to push the play button again. Maybe I haven't been the greatest boyfriend in the world, but you can't deny that I've been pretty great in that I take you out to eat a lot, and to movies and concerts and stuff like that. (I know that you would argue that I get the concert tickets for free cuz of my dad, but I still have to go through the effort of e-mailing his assistant to get them, which can be time-consuming.) Anyway, I guess what I'm trying to say is that I know that you're really into all that romantic stuff like flowers and love e-mails and iTunes mix playlists—stuff that I personally consider a waste of money and time, but whatever, it's a free country and everyone's entitled to their own opinion. And what I was thinking was that instead of making fun of it all the time, maybe I could try and do more of that, especially if it makes you happy.

The truth of the matter is this: I miss you, Sophie. A lot. It might be because of the antibiotics I'm on, but I don't think so. And to show you how serious

I am about the fact that I really do care about you, I'm going to come to Florida and ask you in person to be my girlfriend again. In all honesty it's not like that part was my idea. But I'm not contagious anymore and my mom says that I'm now at the point where I'm really annoying her because I've been cooped up inside the house too long, so she went ahead and convinced the airline to let me use my ticket at no extra cost so she can have some peace and quiet for the next few days. I figured if I'm going to be there, then asking you in person would be a nice touch.

I get in tonight, so if it's not too late by the time I get to my grandmother's condo, maybe we can hang out and watch TV. But knowing how slow my grandmother drives, it might be.

I guess that's it.

Love,

Michael

I couldn't believe it. "Red?" It sounded like Jack was talking underwater. "Red? You okay?"

I just kept staring at the e-mail—mostly at the "Love, Michael" part. The entire time we dated, I could count the number of e-mails I had received from Michael on one hand. Usually, they were always texts, and they were always signed, "Peace, M." But this—this was like . . . a novel. And it was signed, "Love"!

"You look all clammy and stuff," Jack said, reaching for a handful of Doritos. "Here," he said, trying to shove them into my mouth. "Maybe you need some protein."

What was I going to do? I had one guy who had just sent me the longest e-mail he had ever written in his entire life about how in love with me he was (okay, maybe it didn't say it in the actual *e-mail*), and I was sitting next to another guy who—although the *L* word hadn't come up yet there either—basically had made his feelings clear the night he told me I was like a hearty stew.

This was *official* drama. But it didn't feel anything like I thought it would. In books or movies, there's only a certain amount of drama at a time. But this was my life, and I couldn't control how much was rushing at me, like the spigot that controlled it was broken. I pushed his hand away. "No, it's okay. But thanks, that's very sweet."

"What's the matter then?" he asked.

"Uh, nothing," I replied, trying as nonchalantly as possible to close out the e-mail. "I just . . . got an e-mail from . . . my friend Jordan," I said. Or rather, *lied*.

"Oh," he said. Not only was I a woman torn between two lovers; I was a *liar* torn between two lovers. Not exactly something to put on the "special talents" part of my college applications.

"The guy she's seeing . . . he just told her that . . . he really misses her," I went on nervously, lying some more. Funny how it just got easier and easier with each lie. "Well,

174

he said he misses her, but that was just code for 'I'm madly in love with you and have been for the last three years and can't live without you now that you're gone.'" I had no idea where that came from.

Jack had already gone back to watching Reynaldo and Savannah go at it on top of the dining room table, so he didn't answer.

"I'll be right back," I announced, peeling myself off the plastic couch. Again, he didn't notice. That was one of the things I really loved about Jack: his ability to stay so *focused* on things.

As nonchalantly as I could, I walked—then ran—to the bathroom and locked the door. *Omigod, omigod, omigod*, I chanted mentally, scrolling down my phonebook until I hit Jordan's number. When it immediately went to voice mail, I tried her landline.

It was ringing. I tried to take deep breaths, but they were coming out more like combination gulp/hiccups. Was my throat closing up? Could stress send you into ana-phylactic shock? Why wasn't she answering the phone? I hadn't factored in the idea that Michael would actually fight for me. Sure, maybe I did in the movies I played on the screen of my mind as I fell asleep at night, but not, you know, in *real life*.

"Hello?" the voice on the other end of the line said.

"Lulu? This is Sophie," I said, rubbing at my suddenly itchy eyes. Wait a minute—was I having an allergic reac-tion to the drama?

"Sophie! Lovebug, how *are* you?!" she squealed. "I so enjoyed our chat a few weeks ago. I find it very helpful to spend quality time with my fans—"

I didn't have time for small talk. "Yeah, well, is Jordan around?"

"No, honey. She's out with that vegan boy. You don't know how relieved I am. I was starting to think she might be a lesbian," she confided. "Wait a minute—maybe Devon should fall for a *woman* in the next book—"

"Okay, well, if you could just tell her I called," I said quickly, about to hang up.

"Wait, wait—she told me you met a boy on the plane. Tell me *everything*!" she begged.

I was still feeling betrayed about the fact that she was a hypocrite and didn't believe in romance, but I was so desperate that I was at the point where I was ready to ask my grandmother for advice. Plus, even if Lulu didn't believe in true love, she did *write* about it for a living and made enough money off it so that she could shop at Neiman Marcus all she wanted. That had to count for something.

"Look at that—you're being *fought* over!" she exclaimed after I told her the story. "It's like when the Afghani soldier turned performance artist and the hedge fund manager from Connecticut came to blows over Devon at that Manhattan nightclub in my book *Flummoxed by Frisson*."

"I know, but what am I supposed to do?!" I cried. "I've never had this happen to me before."

I heard her light a cigarette. "Oh, honey, that's *easy*. Just call your psychic. That's what I always do when I'm having trouble deciding between two men. If you don't have one, I'll give you the number for mine." She exhaled. "Her name is Lasha and she's *phe-nom-e-nal*. Except don't let her talk you into paying extra to remove any spells. That part's just made up."

"But . . . what about searching my heart? Isn't that what Devon always does when it comes to this stuff?" I asked. I examined my arm. Were those *hives*?

Lulu snorted. "Oh, sweetie. You're such a romantic. I just *love* that. It's so *darling*. I guess you could spend the time doing that, but it sounds like time's of the essence with this one, so you probably want to choose a method that's a little more scientifically proven, don't you agree?"

Since when had psychics become scientifically proven?

"Why do you think my books are so successful?" Lulu continued. "It's in my contract that my publisher has to consult with Lasha first before deciding on a final publication date, so that the book isn't released when Mercury's in retrograde or during a full moon lunar eclipse or anything like that."

That was it. I decided that Lulu was officially nuts. "Um, thanks for the advice, but I think my grandmother's calling me," I said.

"Okay. Well, I hope I was helpful."

"Oh, totally," I said. Maybe not with advice about guys,

but definitely in making it clear that she was completely insane. "If you could tell Jordan I called, that would be great."

"Will do, honey. Have fun. Ta-ta now."

After I hung up, I stared at myself in the bathroom mirror. My eyes were red and swollen. My arm was covered in hives. I was a woman torn between two men. I was being fought over. I was barely recognizable to myself.

My iPhone buzzed.

Dear Sophie,

So have you decided what you want to do yet? Knowing how addicted you are to your iPhone, I'm sure you already read my other e-mail, and frankly, I'm kind of surprised you haven't written back yet. I'd really like to hear back from you as soon as possible, because if you're not interested in getting back together, I'm going to text Warren Bernstein and see if he wants to hang out because he's down there visiting his grandmother too.

Love,

Michael

Oh. My. God. Two "loves" in fifteen minutes? And no "Yo, what up's"? He really *had* changed!

I knew I owed him an answer, but I was completely blanking on what to say.

I heard the front door open. "Kids, we're back!" Grandma Roz boomed.

"If it isn't my favorite senior citizen," I heard Jack drawl.

"Oh, Jack," she giggled. "Are you hungry, *bubelah*?"

"Is a frog green?" I heard Jack drawl, setting her off into another round of giggles.

How could I give up a guy who was able to make an old woman giggle like that? The guilt I felt about even *considering* taking Michael back brought on another round of itching.

I splashed some cold water on my face and patted it dry on one of the two-doves-kissing hand towels. When I walked out, I found Grandma Roz fixing Jack an onion bagel with lox and whitefish. "I was just telling Jack that Art suggested we split up so us girls can go to the beauty parlor while they do something manly like go to the track," she said. "How does that sound, Sophie?"

"*I* think it sounds great," said Jack. "Because I've been hanging around here like white on rice this whole week, you two haven't really had any alone time to bond."

"That's okay," I said, maybe a little too quickly.

"No, really—you came all the way down here to see your grandma, and I've been taking up all your time," he said in between bites of his bagel. After he was done, he shook his head and patted his stomach. "Roz, I swear, you're the best cook this side of the Mississippi. Between

179

your brisket and the way you put just the exact amount of cream cheese on the bagel?" He shook his head. "That English dude on the food channel has nothing on you!"

"Oh, go on," she said, swatting him on the arm and turning red like she always did when he complimented her.

He stood up and brought his plate to the sink. "A day at the beauty parlor sounds like it'd be perfect for you two. Not that either of you need any help in that department."

Grandma Roz patted her head. There was so much hair spray in her hair, it didn't even move. "I *am* due for a wash and set," she said. She turned to me. "What do you say, Sophie? Do you want to come to Arturo's Chateau of Beauty with me? You could get a manicure while I get my hair done."

I had gone to Arturo's Chateau of Beauty the last time I came to visit, and the manicurist's hand shook so much she ended up making my cuticles look like I was starring in a horror movie.

"In fact," she said, waddling over to the file cabinet, "I think I have a coupon." After rifling around, she gasped. "Look at that—it's your lucky day! For the entire month of April, they're running a "Princess for a Day" special: manicure, pedicure, wash, set, *and* makeup application for only $59.99." She looked at me and smiled. "Would you like to be a princess for a day, Sophela? It's a splurge, I know, but you can consider it an early graduation gift."

This was not my grandmother. It was like the "cheap"

chip had been surgically removed ever since Jack came into the picture. "That's really nice, Grandma, but you don't have to do that," I said quickly. "I was thinking maybe I should try and get a little studying done for this trig test I have the week I get back." Wow. Once I started lying, I couldn't stop. The lies were just pouring out of me. What I *really* wanted to do was some Googling about whether there were any documented cases of physical reactions to drama.

"Oh, Sophie, you need to lighten up a little bit!" Grandma Roz clucked. "Have some fun. You know, walk on the wild side every once in a while!" I nearly did a double take. Who was this lady?

"That's exactly what I keep telling her, Roz," Jack said with a sigh. He reached over and squeezed my hand. "Go on, Red. Go have a day of beauty so I can take you out on the town tonight."

So he could take me out, or so I could take him out and add it to his tab? From the looks of things, I could tell they weren't going to let up.

"Okay. Fine. I'll take a walk on the wild side," I replied, getting my purse. Plus, it would give me a chance to finally paint my nails with Dark as Midnight.

If they only knew how wild my life already was. Scratch that. It wasn't wild . . . it was *epic*. A little more than a week ago, my biggest decision was whether to start with my chemistry or my English homework. Then I had become an Urban Dictionary definition, been put on pause, and had ridden on a motorcycle. Now I was torn between two men.

How much wilder could it get?

My iPhone buzzed again.

Dear Sophie,

You there?

Love,

Michael

Talk about an e-mail—or three—that could change your life.

ten

An hour later I was sitting across from Gladys, the manicurist, with a head full of curlers, my cowboy hat safely beside me. It seemed that every woman over the age of sixty in the greater Boca Raton area wanted to be a princess for a day, because when we got there, Arturo's was packed. I had tried to tell Rafi, the cornrowed, half-Cuban/half-Dominican "fabulousness operator" (according to the sign over his chair) that I was into a more natural look, but he had this way of selectively understanding English and just muttered in Spanish as he curled away.

"Grandma, can I ask you a question?" I asked impulsively as I massaged my neck with my free hand. Who knew curlers could be so heavy?

She glanced over from where she was getting her manicure. "What?"

"Remember a few days ago you brought up Jean-Pierre?"

Underneath the bronzer that always gave her an orange glow, like one of those people you read about who OD'd on carrots, I could see her start to pale. "Yeah?"

"You never finished the story. What happened with him?" I asked.

She pointed at the three bottles of nail polish on the table: Pale Pink, Icy Pearl, and Neon Blue. "What color are you going to get?" she asked, flustered. "Personally, I like the Icy Pearl." I had never seen her so nervous.

"Do you have Dark as Midnight?" I asked Gladys.

She shook her head. "Nope. Every time we get a bottle in, someone rips it off."

Yet again I was at a turning point. Was I going to keep making the same safe choices—whether it was nail polish or boys—or was I finally going to take a risk?

"So what ended up happening with Jean-Pierre?" I asked again, my hand hovering about the three bottles.

She sighed. "What happened was over the course of three weeks he touched my heart at its very center," Grandma Roz said, "at its very *core*—awakening in me a passion I never knew existed—and then . . . I went back to your grandfather and my suburban housewife existence full of carpooling and bridge games and low-cholesterol chicken recipes."

Wait . . . what? I put the polish choosing on hold and turned to her.

"C'mon, sweetie, pick a color. I don't have all day," Gladys said, annoyed.

184

Grandma Roz sighed. "He did give me the candelabras as a parting gift."

I gasped even louder. "But I thought those were Greene family heirlooms that had been brought over from Poland by a mule!"

She shook her head. "No. I made that part up. Didn't want to set a bad example for your father by letting him think his mother was a hussy." She shrugged. "Lately, I've been thinking a lot about Jean-Pierre—probably because I have so little time left, you know—and how alive he made me feel. That's why I wanted the candelabras."

Who knew Grandma Roz was a romantic?!

She shook her head sadly. "I got a letter from him about a year later. He had fallen in love with an Italian fashion designer, and they were in the process of opening up a bed-and-breakfast in Tuscany."

I looked up from the nail polish bottles. "After such an incredible connection like that, he fell in love with another woman?"

"The fashion designer was a man."

"He turned out to be *gay*?" I gasped again.

She shrugged again. "I hate to be the one to tell you, but that sort of thing happens more often than you would think."

That was true. A girl named Cindy Gold at my school had fallen for her SAT tutor, only to find out he was gay. But then she ended up with Adam Silver, a total hottie, so no one felt too bad for her. But this . . . this was a different

185

story—this was my grandmother. My velour-tracksuit-wearing, Mylanta-drinking grandmother had a *past*. Not just a past, but a pretty torrid past. And no one knew! I didn't even want to think of what else she was hiding.

"But if he touched you so deeply—if he made you feel so *alive*—then why did you go back to Grandpa Max?" I asked. As much as Michael's e-mail had made me realize that I really did miss him, I didn't know if I could give up the feeling of freedom I had felt when riding around on the motorcycle with Jack.

She shot me a withering look. "You mean, just because every time Jean-Pierre looked at me and I felt little electric shocks on the bottom of my feet, why didn't I give up my entire life as I knew it and uproot my son and move to a foreign country where I barely spoke the language so I could live with a man whose mood swings were off the charts and who liked to start arguments over the littlest things just so we could then have make-up sex? And to top it all off, he likes men?"

I cringed. Talk about TMI. "Okay, I guess when you put it that way, the pros don't exactly outweigh the cons," I agreed, "but what about the touching-your-heart part? That's, like, *huge*."

For probably only the fourth time in all my sixteen years on the planet that I could remember, Grandma Roz took my hand in hers. "Sophie, I'm about to share with you the single most important piece of advice you're ever going to get. Not only is it going to save you a lot of heartache, but it'll keep you off the couch of one of those overpriced headshrinkers like your mom. Are you ready?"

I nodded.

"You sure?"

I nodded again.

She leaned in and looked around to make sure that no one was listening. "A man should always love you just a *little* bit more than you love him," she whispered.

"Huh?"

She rolled her eyes. "What am I, speaking Yiddish? I *said* a man should always love you just a little bit more than you love him. Those—what do you call them?—*hotties*, like Jack and Jean-Pierre? Sure, they're exciting and every girl should experience them at least once, but when it comes time to settle down, you want to be with someone like Grandpa Max or Art."

I sighed. Sure, other than the few times I caught him staring at other girls when we were out, Jack had been faithful, but what if the stray dog thing kicked in when got back to L.A.? I could only imagine what kind of allergic reaction I'd have to *that* kind of drama. But as I imagined myself fifty years from now with a guy like Art who jiggled the change in his pocket, I shuddered. "But I thought you liked Jack?"

"I do. He's a very nice boy. That being said, I hate to tell you this, but I don't think he's the kind of guy who'll hold your hair back from your face when you're bent over the toilet with food poisoning or go to the pharmacy at midnight to get you feminine napkins or Rolaids," she replied. "That Michael, though—he would."

As if he were psychic, my iPhone buzzed again with another e-mail from Michael.

Dear Sophie,
Okay, I get that I've been kind of a jerk, but it's rude to just ignore a person's e-mails like this.
Love,
Michael

I flashed back to the time that I got sick from a burrito at Michael's house. While he hadn't hung out in the bathroom with me while I puked my guts up, he *did* go to 7-11 and get me some ginger ale to help my stomach. But did that mean he loved me a little bit more than I loved him, or did it just mean he was afraid I was going to hurl in his just-washed car when he drove me home? I'm not sure if Jack would've gone to get me ginger ale. If he did, though, I knew I'd be the one who paid for it.

I had thought I was destined for an Excitement-with-a-capital-*E* life, but maybe a small *e* life could be okay too. Well, a small *e* with a couple of big *E* moments thrown in there.

Gladys stood up, pulling her too-short shirt down over

her leopard-print leggings. "Since you're going to take your time like this, I'm gonna go have a smoke. Maybe when I get back you'll have made your decision."

"Take it from me—those stray dogs may get your heart pumping," Grandma Roz continued, "which, at my age, is a good thing, but you're going to end up spending all your time worrying about how to get that one foot they always have out the door back into the room. Chemistry is important, but it's not the *only* thing."

Did *everyone* know about this stray dog thing except for me?

I thought about it for a moment. "But the stable ones," I said, "they're just so . . ."

"Boring?" Grandma Roz suggested.

"Well . . . *yeah*." I had to admit, getting all these e-mails from Michael was a thrill, but if I got back together with him, I'd bet anything he'd go back to his super-short texts.

She shrugged. "They may be, but unlike the other ones, you can depend on them to stick around for more than a month and be there for you through the tough times. Which means that you have a chance of it turning into a real relationship instead of just being a hot, passionate fling that burns out, like the ones that Delilah girl's always having."

"Who's Delilah?"

"The girl in those books you like."

"Devon," I corrected.

She shrugged. "Delilah, Devon. All those *shiksas* sound alike to me. The point is, do you want to end up like her? Running around the world like a chicken with her head cut off, having meaningless affairs with men who refuse to grow up and settle down? You think she sleeps well at night?"

I shrugged. She *did* have superexpensive, thousand-thread count sheets and fancy silk nightgowns. And took sleeping pills.

"Take it from me, Sophie—she doesn't," Grandma Roz said, waving her now-pearl-painted nails around. "I'm old. I know these things. Devon is *miserable*. She feels empty inside, especially during the holidays when everyone is with their families and she's sharing a Lean Cuisine with that little dog of hers."

"How do you know about Miu Miu?" I asked suspiciously.

She looked down. "So maybe I've picked up one or two of your books over the years when I've come to visit," she admitted. "I can't remember everything I read—I'm an old woman, for crying out loud. But the point is, sometimes you have to sit through the boring parts to get to the good parts."

Gladys came back and sat down, reeking of cigarettes. "Did ya decide?"

I stared at my choices. Was I going to continue being a Cotton Candy girl—spending my Saturday nights with Michael, who fifty years from now would be jiggling his change in his pocket like Art? Or was I going to finally bite the bullet and live on the wild side with Jack—but with the stress of worrying that at any minute my stray dog might bolt?

"I'll go with . . . the blue," I finally said.

"The *blue*?" said Grandma Roz. "What are you, crazy?"

I shrugged. Apparently so.

Once Rafi was done with my hair and makeup, I looked like an extra in *The Sopranos*, this TV show that Dad used to watch about people in the Mafia. Not only was I about three inches taller once he teased my hair out, but my face was itching from the makeover, complete with blue eye shadow to match my nails. I could already tell it was going to leave me with a war zone of pimples.

"I sure hope you have a hot date tonight, *chica*," he said as he finished painting my lips with what felt like glue. "Cuz you are *muy caliente*, baby. Believe me, if I were buyin' what you're sellin' I'd be all over you."

It may have just been a bribe so that I wouldn't blab the truth about the candelabras to my parents, but after we were done at Arturo's, Grandma Roz took me to the mall to buy me a new outfit for my big night out with Jack.

After convincing her that while, yes, Talbots had some cute things, I'd probably have more luck at Always 16, we

191

made plans to meet at the food court a half hour later so that she could go to Bed Bath & Beyond and use the coupon that had come in the mail that morning to buy a new humidifier.

"Sophie?" I heard a voice say as I debated between a Jack-like pleather jacket to go with my new boots (I had barely taken them off since Jack got them for me, even though they made my shins sweat) and a Michael-approved red and white polka-dotted sundress.

I looked up to see Juliet DeStefano, holding the very same black tank top I had been pondering just five minutes before. "Juliet! What are you doing in Florida?!" I said. Omigod, I couldn't believe I was talking to Juliet DeStefano. Was she on the run again? Was she even going by the name Juliet anymore, or had she changed it?

"Visiting my grandmother," she replied.

Juliet DeStefano had a *grandmother*? Who lived in *Florida*?

"I'm visiting *my* grandmother too!" I cried. Now that my life was on the dramatic side, we had a lot more in common than I thought. "So what have you been doing?" Maybe her grandmother was really young, and they got all dressed up and went and sat in hotel bars and tried to bilk lonely men out of millions of dollars like the women in this movie I had once seen on Lifetime.

"Oh, we're having a great time. Last night she taught me how to knit, and the day before that we played bingo at the community room in her condo complex."

I searched her face to see if she was being sarcastic, but she just smiled like an actress in a feminine hygiene product commercial. "Oh. Wow. That sounds . . . fun," I said. Most of the guys in the Boca Raton area were retired, but I would've thought the ones our age would be falling at her feet and fighting to take her out to chain restaurants every night. "But I bet when you're not knitting, you're probably hanging out at the pools, where all the boys visiting their grandmothers are fighting over who can put sunblock on your back." What was I talking about? Juliet DeStefano didn't use sunblock—she probably used baby oil.

"No, I don't go in the sun," she replied. "I burn super easily."

"Oh," I said, disappointed. But now that I looked at her a little more closely, I saw that she was a little on the pasty side. Not only that, but her long brown hair looked to be on the thin side. "But you probably take cool day trips to, like, the alligator races and stuff like that, huh?"

She shook her head. "No. We went to the movies the other night, though. The one based on the latest Nicholas Sparks book. And then we went to Olive Garden afterward. That was fun."

"I *love* Nicholas Sparks!" I gasped. "He's my second favorite author." I was dying to see that movie. I looked at my watch. "Speaking of food, I have to go meet my grandmother in the food court now."

She looked at hers. I would've thought it was encrusted

with diamonds, but it was just a plain old run-of-the-mill Seiko. "I have to meet mine there too."

When we got to the food court, we discovered that the two women knew each other from the mah-jongg circuit. I don't know what I expected, but I couldn't get over how *grandmotherly* Juliet's grandmother looked, with her lavender sweatshirt that said MY GRANDCHILDREN WENT TO SAN DIEGO AND ALL I GOT WAS THIS LOUSY SWEATSHIRT and her pink velour jogging pants. Not only that, but the way she looked at Juliet was so *sweet*. Exactly how you'd think a grandmother would look.

"We'll let you girls eat while we browse in Chico's," Grandma Roz said.

"Okay," I said. While they were gone, I could pick Juliet's brain a little. Maybe my life was more dramatic than hers at the moment, but if anyone could give me advice about what to do about guys, it was Juliet.

After we settled ourselves at a table with our Mexican food, Juliet took out a prescription pill bottle and twisted the top off. Oh my god, she was taking pills right in the middle of the mall. I choked back my gasp.

Was Juliet a drug addict? Was it to kill the pain of having to live a life of lies and go on the run? Devon had been addicted to pills for a while, but thankfully went to rehab, in *Addled by Addiction*, the one where she fell madly in love with a fellow rehabber who had been a big rock star in the eighties. Wait—maybe Juliet was manic depressive

194

like Devon's sister, Cassandra, and it was for that, so she wouldn't stay up for three days in a row and then start taking off her clothes in the middle of Sunset Boulevard because she was so overtired that she thought a rain puddle was a swimming pool. That's what happened in *Insane with Instability*.

I wasn't sure if I should ask what they were, but since I was now living my life on the edge, I steeled my courage. "What is that?" I asked, pointing at the bottle.

"It's Prevacid," she replied, as she popped one in her mouth and washed it down with some Diet Coke. "It's for my ulcer," she explained. "I have to take it before I eat. Especially when I have spicy food."

Oh. "I thought only old people got ulcers," I said.

She shook her head. "My shrink says that lots of people who suffer from anxiety get it."

Was I the only one in our class who didn't go to a shrink?

"Hey, I heard you were going to Mexico with Jordan," she said as she crunched on a tortilla chip. It's funny, I had never noticed how crooked her teeth were.

"I was, but then it got cancelled, and I had to bring these candelabras to my grandmother that I thought were family heirlooms but that turned out to be from a French guy she had a fling with."

"Wow . . . that sounds *exciting*," she said, impressed. I had impressed Juliet DeStefano! I was carrying on a

195

conversation with her! It was almost like she was . . . normal. Who would have figured?

Hmm. Had her forehead always been broken out like that? Now that Juliet had suddenly become a normal human being, I felt so much closer to her. Which is why I broke down and told her everything. Well, that and the fact that drama wasn't very fun if you didn't get to share it with anyone.

"And my boyfriend, Michael, was going to come and visit his grandmother too, but then he couldn't because he got the chicken pox." I reached for a chip. "And then soon after he pushed the pause button on our relationship, I met Jack on the plane," I said, shoving more chips in my mouth. Just *thinking* about everything I had been through over the last week zapped my energy and made me hungry. "And then Michael decided to go from pause to stop," I said, my mouth full. "Which wasn't so bad, because then I could kiss Jack and not feel guilty."

"Omigod," she gasped. "Your life is like a novel or something!"

I told her about Jack buying me the motorcycle boots as a token of his love (she thought they were really cool) and the e-mail from Michael professing his love—even about Jean-Pierre. After I was done, I realized Juliet was right—my life *was* like a book. And now, instead of being something you'd find in the middle-grade section, it was something you'd find in adult fiction.

"So what do you think I should do about Michael and Jack?" I said, trying to catch my breath. "I mean, with all the boyfriends you've had, I'm sure you've been fought over tons of times."

"What boyfriends?" she asked, taking a bite of her taco.

I took a sip of my soda. "Well . . . all the ones . . . you've had . . ." Now that I thought about it, I didn't know for sure that she had a bunch, but she had to have had a few. She was Juliet DeStefano!

"I've only had one," she replied. "Doug Barrington. My freshman year in Atlanta. For three weeks."

"Okay, but what about the guys you've, you know—"

"Supposedly hooked up with?" she said bitterly. "Like the guys on the football team?"

"Well, uh . . . yeah," I replied. "And, you know, the ones on the soccer team."

She rolled her eyes. "Now they're saying it's the soccer team too? Great."

"Wait—so you're not—"

"The Castle Heights junior-class slut?" she asked.

I gave a shrod, which is a half-shrug/half-nod. Obviously, I wouldn't have used that S-word, but well, yeah.

"No. I'm not."

In light of everything else I had discovered about her in the last half hour, I guess that shouldn't have surprised me.

But still, even with the grandmother, the ulcer, and everything, it was still hard to think of her as just normal.

"Maybe because once I went out for pizza with Bobby Newman, and afterward he tried to maul me until I told him that I had a black belt in Ashtanga and would snap his neck in two if he didn't stop."

"Isn't Ashtanga a form of yoga?" I asked.

"Yeah. But he's so stupid, he didn't know that," she replied. "And when he found out he was pretty pissed."

I laughed. Who knew Juliet liked to knit *and* was funny?

"Or maybe it's because I have big boobs?" she went on.

I glanced at her tank top. They *were* pretty big.

"I know it makes me sound lame, but I've never done anything more than kissed a guy," she confessed as she daintily dabbed at the corners of her mouth. "So as much as I'd like to help you, I have no idea what you should do." She sighed. "You're so lucky, Sophie—I wish *my* life were that exciting. Before the French club calendar, my life was as boring as it gets." She sighed again. "I know I got voted in for every month as a joke, but at least now I have *something* to look forward to."

I knew just what she meant. That's exactly what I used to say whenever I heard Lulu had a new book coming out!

Wait—had Juliet DeStefano just said she wished she had *my* life?

I reached down and pinched my thigh. "Ow," I said aloud. I guess she had. "Can I ask you a question?"

"Sure," she replied.

"Is your name really Juliet?"

She gave me a weird look. "Yeah. Why?"

I shrugged. "Never mind." So much for thinking I had other people all figured out.

After lunch, Juliet and I went back to Always 16, where I helped her pick out some outfits for the calendar. Now that we had kind of become friends, I wasn't bitter any-more about the calendar situation. (Although I had to admit that with a few of the things she chose, when she said, "Does this make my butt look big?" and I said no, it was a *teeny* bit of a lie.) As we said good-bye (she and her grandmother were heading off to Color Me Mine to paint some pottery) we exchanged e-mails and numbers so we could hang out when we got back to L.A.

"The boys still must be out," Grandma Roz said when we got back to the Garden of Eden and saw that Art's Cadillac wasn't in its parking spot with the orange cones he used to make sure no one got within six feet of it.

But when we got inside the condo, Jack was there, in the living room, surrounded by files that said things like "stock statements" and "bond statements" and a big enve-lope that said TeePeeMatic, the company that made my great-grandfather a millionaire. I saw broken glass on the

199

floor, and a shattered window behind him. Jack turned when he heard us come in, and looked really freaked out.

"*Oy gevalt!*" Grandma Roz bellowed, dropping her bags. "What's going on here?!"

I dropped mine too, and my hand immediately clutched at my heart. "Yeah! What's going on here?" Obviously, spending time with Grandma Roz had rubbed off on me.

"I don't know," Jack cried. "Right after you left, Mervyn, the motorcycle guy, texted me to say I could come pick up the bike, so instead of going to the track with Art, I took the bus to the trailer park where he lives. But the bike was *not* as advertised on eBay and was completely covered with rust—you can bet I'm contacting customer service about that seller—and when I got back, I found the window broken and all this stuff on the floor!"

"Oy, my heart. This just might be the one that puts me six feet under," Grandma Roz moaned as she waddled over to the fake Picasso painting on the wall and took it down.

"What are you doing?" I asked.

"Checking the safe," she replied, matter-of-factly.

There was a safe?! First the candelabras, and now this. What other secrets was I going to find out about my grandmother—that she had had a baby before my dad and gave it up for adoption?

When she twirled the lock and the door popped open, Jack whistled. "Man, check out all those jewelry boxes."

I turned to him, the hair on the back of my neck standing

up. He couldn't possibly have had anything to do with the break-in . . . right?

She counted the boxes. "Oy, thank God they're all here." She opened a blue velvet one. "Ah, the diamond and sapphire earrings that Juan Carlo gave me—I don't know what I'd do if I lost those."

"Who's Juan Carlo?" I asked.

She looked up. "He was a . . . friend," she replied. "You don't know him. It was before Art came into the picture."

Another guy? How many boyfriends did she have? I peered over her shoulder into the safe. I could see that in addition to the jewelry boxes, there were two silver menorahs. "Did you get the menorahs from 'friends' as well?" I asked suspiciously. This woman wasn't my grandmother—she was a stranger.

She shrugged. "What can I tell you? I'm quite the catch at the Garden of Eden." She walked over to the phone. "I'm going to call the police and file a report."

I started walking through the condo to check if any other windows were broken. I couldn't believe how calm Grandma was—I was feeling shaky, but she was calm as could be. In between rooms, I'd peer into the living room to see what Jack was doing, but by this time he was settled on the couch watching *Wheel of Fortune*. "Everything else looks okay," I called out.

"The important thing is that you're okay, Jack," Grandma Roz called out from the kitchen. "You must be hungry after all that drama, so right after I make this call, I'm going to go make you a bagel."

"Yeah, a little something would be nice," I heard him call out.

When I walked back into the living room, the TV was still on, but he wasn't on the couch anymore. Instead he was standing in front of the safe, which was still open.

"What are you doing?" I demanded.

He jumped and whipped around. "Man, Red, you scared me."

Did he look *guilty*, or was he just *startled*? Something wasn't adding up. Jack still hadn't paid me back for anything so far, but that didn't mean he was a criminal, did it?

Or was this just like in *Drowning in Doubt*, when Devon found out that the rabbi she had fallen in lust with was actually a thief? If I remembered correctly, *he* stole silver menorahs too!

"What's the matter?" he asked.

"Uh, nothing," I replied, glad I remembered from all those *CSI* episodes I had watched with Jeremy that the most important thing to do when around a criminal was to not let on that you knew they were a criminal. As nonchalantly as I could, I shut the safe and started picking up the stock certificates.

He walked over and put his arms around me. "You sure? You're looking at me kind of weird."

"Weird how?" I asked, nervously.

He shrugged. "Most of the time you look at me like you're all into me, but now . . . I don't know . . . it's different." A panicked look came over his face. "You still like me, right? What you said last night when we were making out—that I'm the coolest guy you've ever met in your entire life—that still stands, right?"

For someone who never worried because he always lived in the moment, he sounded completely freaked out. Almost like he was . . . insecure.

"Right, Red?" he said, anxiously.

Before I could respond, my iPhone rang. I glanced at the display. It was Michael! What was I going to do? I couldn't take the call in front of Jack. Maybe he was a criminal, but that didn't mean he deserved to be kicked when he was was feeling so unsure of himself.

Except that he had totally lost interest in me and was back on the couch watching TV.

"You're supposed to be on a plane!" I whispered when I answered.

"Why haven't you responded to any of my e-mails?" he demanded.

"I've been busy. Wait—you're not using your phone when all electronic devices are supposed to be turned off, are you?"

"No. I'm already here in Florida. I got on an earlier flight. Hey, Sophie, you're not really mad at me, are you?" he asked nervously.

I rolled my eyes. I wasn't one of those girls who liked to play games, but it was obvious that the best way to get a guy to like you was to pretend you weren't interested. "Can I call you back in a little while? I'm sort of in the middle of something," I said.

Right then Jack sneezed. Maybe *he* was allergic to drama too.

"Is that your grandmother?" Michael asked.

"It's the TV," I said as I marched into the bathroom.

"Wait—where are you going?" Jack called after me. "Are you *sure* you're not mad at me?"

As I stared at my arms, I could see the red welts starting to come back. I couldn't take the stress anymore. Living an exciting life torn between two men was literally making me sick. Or at least very, very itchy. It was time for me to stop being what Devon's sister called a "sneaky, conniving harlot" and return to my regular-girl roots. I sighed. "Michael, there's something I need to tell you," I said, scratching at my arm.

"What is it?"

"Well, I was very moved by the declarations of love you sent me today—"

"I didn't say I loved you," he said.

"Yes you did. You wrote 'Love, Michael.'"

"Yeah, but that's just a . . . whaddyacallit . . . salutation."

"Actually, it's a closing salutation," I corrected. "Okay,

maybe you didn't say you *loved* me," I admitted, "but you *did* say you wanted to get back together."

"Do we really need to spend so much time talking about this?" he asked, uncomfortably. "Why does everything always need to be such a *discussion*?"

I ignored him and continued. "But the thing is, during the time when we were broken up, I—"

"Sophie, do you want a bagel too?" Grandma Roz yelled from the kitchen.

"No, thank you," I yelled back.

"*Ow.* My ear!" Michael yelled.

"Sorry. Anyway, after we broke up . . . around the same time, actually . . . I met someone," I admitted. "And . . . well, let's just say it got pretty serious pretty quickly." I felt horrible breaking his heart like this, but I had to stop spinning a web of lies. It was such a relief to finally come clean after holding my secret in for so long that my legs buckled and I had to sit on the toilet.

"What do you mean, you met someone?" Michael asked, confused. "You've been in Florida with old people."

I scratched at my other arm. "I met him on the plane. His name is Jack. And, actually, he *is* a little older. And very well-traveled. He's in a band. They've toured all over the Midwest." I decided to leave out the part about him maybe being a criminal until I gathered more information.

"But we were together for three *years*!" Michael said. "You can't just hook up with someone and in three *days*

205

say it's serious without giving me a chance. What kind of return policy is *that*?"

I had forgotten how funny Michael could be. Jack was hot, but he wasn't all that funny. And funny *was* very important.

"Do you at least want something to drink?" Grandma Roz yelled. "I just made a new batch of Crystal Light!"

"No, I'm okay," I yelled back.

"*Ow*," Michael yelled.

"Sorry."

"Do you yell in *his* ear and shatter *his* eardrums too?" he demanded. I could tell from the sound of his voice that not only was he heartbroken, but he was also seething with jealousy, just like Juergen, the German architect in *Reveling in Rapture*, after Devon left him for a Hungarian violinist.

The stress of shattering Michael's heart like this was so overwhelming I almost started hyperventilating. As I grabbed onto the side of the toilet to steady myself, I flushed it by mistake.

"What's that noise?" he asked.

"The toilet flushing," I admitted.

"While you've been telling me about how you're cheating on me, you've been going to the *bathroom*?!"

"Okay, A) I was not cheating on you—I didn't kiss him until you decided to 'push the stop button'; and B) I pushed the toilet thingy by mistake," I said. "I just wanted to have this conversation in private because my grandmother and

Jack are in the living room. Probably watching *The Sands of Time*."

"What?"

"A soap opera."

"The guy you're cheating on me with watches *soap operas*?!"

My neck started to itch. "Okay, C) he's very in touch with his feminine side because of the musician thing; and D) I repeat—I am not cheating on you. I met him after we had semi-broken up."

"Yeah, but everyone knows that there's a two-week window after a breakup where either party gets to change their mind!" he cried.

There was? Usually, I was so good about Googling stuff, but I had gotten so caught up in Jack, I hadn't had time to double-check the rules.

"I can't believe this," he grumbled. "I flew all the way to Florida to see you—"

"Um, excuse me—you flew to Florida because you were hanging around your house being annoying and your mother couldn't take it anymore," I corrected him.

"You'd think by dating someone for three years, you'd know them pretty well," he went on, "but I guess not. I guess there's nothing else to say then—"

"Michael, wait—" I cried. I couldn't let it end like this. "See, the thing is, as compatible as Jack and I may be, the truth is . . . I'm torn." Especially if it turned out Jack was a thief and the only time I'd be able to see him was during jail visits. "And sometimes I find myself missing you. A lot. Like a lot–a lot." Okay, maybe the missing-him thing hadn't happened until this phone call made me remember how funny he was, but it was definitely the case now.

"Yeah, well, you can't have it both ways," Michael said coldly. "You've made your decision. Anyway, I have to go now. We're about to go into Red Lobster for the early bird special. Good-bye, Sophie. It was nice knowing you."

I opened my mouth to say something, but the line went dead.

No wonder Devon ended up in rehab—the pressure from feeling torn and the guilt of having to break someone's heart was enough to make anyone drink and become addicted to antianxiety medication on top of diet pills.

eleven

I was right—when I came out of the bathroom, Jack and Grandma Roz were watching *The Sands of Time*. Apparently, the drama of a nurse named Monica making out with Dr. Geraldo Alonso, who had to leave his country during a revolution, had replaced the drama of the break-in.

Jack looked up. "You okay, Red? You look a little upset. It's not me, is it?" he asked anxiously.

"No, it's not you," I sighed. Okay—thinking it was always about you? So not sexy. But I *was* upset. I had gotten what I thought I wanted—a free-spirited, motorcycle-driving hottie—but maybe at the end of the day, I *liked* sitting on a couch watching *MTV Cribs* on a Friday night. Or maybe not. I didn't know anymore. Drama really jumbled your brain.

"You kids should go out for your night on the town," Grandma Roz said. I couldn't get over how calm she was about everything. "No reason to sit here on your tushes and watch me fill out a police report. Especially since you're all dolled up after your day of beauty, Sophie."

Unfortunately, with the humidity, all but one of my curls had uncurled and my makeup had pretty much melted down my face.

"Whaddya say, Red? Ready for another adventure?" asked Jack.

"I guess so," I replied. It was either that, or sit there wondering if I had made the wrong decision about breaking up with Michael.

"Where are we going?" I asked a half hour later. Once you got out of the West Palm/Boca Raton area of Florida, there were less orthopedic-sneaker-wearing old people and ALL YOU CAN EAT EARLY BIRD SPECIAL signs and more rusted-out cars on cinder blocks and check-cashing places. On a good day, it was kind of creepy, but when you were in a Buick with a guy who may or may not be a criminal, it bordered on downright scary.

"Not quite sure. Thought we'd just drive for a while. Find a romantic spot and just hang," he said, flashing me a grin.

Not the answer I was hoping for. How could I not have noticed how yellow his teeth were before now? And was it just my imagination, or were they kind of pointy?

My iPhone buzzed.

Just wanted u to know I met someone new 2. So now we're even.

Little bubbles of jealousy began to stir in my stomach. I typed back.

Who is she? A waitress at Red Lobster?

NO. She's a video vixen. I met her at the shuffleboard court.

A VIDEO VIXEN???? YEAH, RIGHT.

She is! She did a 50 Cent video! She's half-Cuban/half-Jewish. Her grandmother lives here. Oh, and she's an older woman—18.

The bubbles began to rise higher.

Yeah, well, Jack's even OLDER. He's 19!

Yeah, well, she once met Beyonce!

The bubbles began to pop.

"Who you texting?" Jack asked as he pushed the preset radio stations looking for a good song. Unfortunately, all that came up was easy listening and classical.

"Just someone . . . stupid," I replied, texting back:

U said you liked my flat butt, but i just KNEW what u really wanted was someone with a booty!

Do your parents know ur hanging out with a guy who rides a motorcycle and only went to community college?????

"Hey look, a Dairy Queen," said Jack. "Wanna stop?"

"Sure," I said, not looking up from the phone. Maybe a Blizzard would help calm the jealousy bubbles that were now burning—like how Grandma Roz took baking soda for her heartburn.

Other than the bored kid behind the counter reading a

Fangoria magazine, we were the only people in the place. The day before I probably would've thought that it was superromantic, but now? I wasn't so sure.

After I had paid for our ice cream and we were settled at a table, Jack sighed and looked at me. "Red, we need to talk."

Oh my god. How many "We need to talk" talks could a girl handle? My arms began to itch again. I was going to have to buy some calamine lotion with the little money I had left.

"About what?"

"Well, any self-help book worth its salt talks about how good communication is key in a relationship, and I'm just feeling . . . I don't know . . . that we're not *communicating* so good lately. Like ever since you got home this afternoon, you've been on Venus and I've been on Mars. Especially after the break-in."

I fiddled with the brim of my cowboy hat. "I don't know what you're talking about," I said nervously.

"I just feel like, I dunno, suddenly you don't *trust* me or something," he continued. "And everyone knows that trust is the most important part of a relationship."

"And humor, that's important too," I added. "And chemistry."

He shrugged. "Well, yeah, but after a while that chemistry stuff settles down. It's just a fact of life. Actually, that's when a relationship and true intimacy *really* begins. Before that is what they call the 'infatuation' phase—when the oxytocin is being released."

"Oxy what?"

"Oxytocin," he repeated. "It's the same hormone that's released when a woman breast-feeds. They call it the 'bonding hormone.'"

Who *was* this guy? What happened to the danger-ous Jack? The one who winked and turned on electronic devices when they were supposed to stay off? What on earth was he talking about? "How do you know this stuff? From your therapist?"

"No, I saw it on a special during a PBS pledge drive." *Jack* watched PBS?

He took my hand. "I know you think I was the one who tried to steal from your grandmother," he said quietly. "I can see it in your eyes. But I didn't. I'd never do anything like that." He shuddered. "I still remember how much my butt hurt after my dad found out I stole a Charleston Chew from the Quick-E-Mart when I was seven. Plus, stealing really screws with your karma."

Self-help books, karma . . . the next thing I knew, Jack was going to tell me he was a Buddhist.

"And while I've come to really, really care about you this past week, Red, I'm not sure I can see a future with someone who would think I could do something like that. Which sucks because I think I'm kind-of-sort-of falling—"

Before he could finish my phone started ringing.

"You gonna get that?" he asked.

I shook my head and turned the ringer off to shut it up. It seemed rude to take a call when someone was about to tell you that they were kind-of-sort-of falling in something with you.

"Kind-of-sort-of falling what?" I asked.

"Huh?"

"You said you were 'kind-of-sort-of falling' something before the phone rang."

He looked confused for a moment. If I had learned anything about Jack over the past few days it was that he had close to zero short-term memory. Finally it clicked. "Oh right. I was about to say that I feel like I'm kind-of-sort-of falling in—"

The phone buzzed.

He sighed. "I gotta tell you, Red. I'm thinking you might end up in rehab because of that thing," he said, pointing to the iPhone.

"I'm ignoring it!" I cried. Although I had to admit that in doing so, I felt like my mom said she felt when she started craving a cigarette—like my head starting buzzing and my heart started beating faster. I couldn't win. My willpower gone, I picked up the phone. "Just—it might be important . . ."

I looked down.

Not that u care or anything, but Carmen and i are going to Pablo's Putt-Putt Palace . . . M.

"Is it important?" he asked.

"*No*," I scoffed.

Before I could stop him, Jack took the phone from me

and read the text. He looked up at me. "Who's Carmen? And who's M?"

I sighed. If Jack could sit across from me and bare his soul and tell me he was kind-of-sort-of falling in something with me, he deserved to know what was going on inside of me. I took a deep breath and told him about my relationship with Michael, about the uncomfortable yet exciting feeling of being torn between two lovers. His eyes started glazing over twenty-five minutes into my confession, so maybe the "honesty" and "communication" he had been talking about didn't have to include every little detail, but I figured it was better to be safe than sorry.

"... and then when he started saying that I was only with you because you were the total polar opposite of him and I was doing it because my parents wouldn't approve—"

Jack looked up from the inchworm he had made with his straw wrapper and raised an eyebrow. "Why wouldn't your parents approve?"

"It's not that they wouldn't *approve*," I said, starting to backpedal. "It's just that, you know, you're ... *different* than the guys I know."

"Because I have an accent and didn't go to some fancy college?" he asked. "You know, I'm sick and tired of people trying to put me in a box and judging me by the way I look and sound," he said angrily, slamming his hand on the inchworm and squashing it. "Ow," he said, wincing.

"I'm not judging you," I said.

"No, but your parents are!"

"But my parents haven't even met you yet," I replied, confused.

"Oh, so now you're so embarrassed of me that you're afraid to introduce me to your parents?" he scoffed.

I felt like this conversation was turning into a very complicated word problem, and I was totally lost.

He stood up. "That's it. We're going to Pablo's Putt-Putt."

"We are?"

He nodded.

"Why?"

"Because I'm going to kick your *boyfriend's* butt," he replied, stomping toward the exit. "C'mon."

I couldn't believe it—Jack was *jealous*, and he was going to fight for my hand! Or at least fight for the right to be the only guy I made out with. So what if Michael wasn't technically my boyfriend anymore; that was just a minor detail.

As we walked back to the car, I thought about how hot Jack looked when he got jealous.

"Red, this is about self-respect and self-esteem and all those other 'self' things," he said.

"Self-respect? Whose? Mine?" I asked, confused.

"Mine!"

I sighed as I opened the door. "So you wouldn't, like, fight for *me*?"

"Well, yeah, of course I would. You're my . . ."

"Girlfriend?" I suggested.

"You know how I feel about labels," he reminded me. "I was going to say you're my Red."

A half hour ago I may have fallen for that line, but now it just sounded super-cheesy. Even though she wasn't supposed to discuss her patients, Mom once told me about a guy who would literally have a choking fit any time he tried to say the word "girlfriend" or would sneeze whenever anyone else used the word. Which meant that for three years, Mom had to use the word "ex-something" when talking about his girlfriends.

"But the thing of it is, you wouldn't want a . . . Jack . . . who let someone disrespect him like that. You'd want a Jack who stood up for himself."

Then it happened.

There had been a few times in my life where suddenly I had a moment where it felt like a veil was being lifted off my face, and I could really *see* someone. It had happened when I was eight, when one day I looked over and saw Jeremy sitting so close to the television that his nose was almost touching the screen, and I realized that he was always going to be weird, but even so, he was always going to be a lot more interesting than my other friends' siblings. Not to mention he could help me with math and organizing. It had happened with Lulu that Sunday when I realized that she was a total hypocrite.

And it happened at that moment with Jack.

Of *course* he was talking about *his* self-respect and *his* self-esteem. Of *course* it was about him. Wasn't it always? How many times did he seem to react to something I had just said, only to then come back and say something about himself? And then there was that conversation yesterday where he was going on and on so much about himself that he didn't even notice I had gotten up and gone to the bathroom, and then he was *still* talking when I got back? With him, it was "The Jack Show" 24/7. Granted he was hot enough to have his own series, but I didn't want to be in a relationship where I was a minor character with only one line. I wanted equal screen time. I deserved equal screen time!

I could sit there and make up as many excuses for him as I wanted: he was just super self-reflective and I was super-generous and that's why we spent so much time talking about him, or he had a bad memory and that's why he never remembered anything that didn't somehow have to do with him. But the truth of the matter was that he was totally self-centered and way too preoccupied with himself to ever be in love with another human being (i.e., me). Not only that—he was a mooch!

And right then, as if by magic, a spell was broken. Jack wasn't a charming, wolfishly hot dream-guy. He was a regular old selfish whatever-guy, and I just wasn't into him anymore.

I felt a little shaky, but oddly free. My soul mate wasn't my soul mate anymore. He was just some *guy*. Mulling over the concept of Jack being anything other than special seemed mathematically impossible at first—like how the plural of "sheep" is "sheep," or the plural of "shrimp" is "shrimp," or the plural of "fish" is "fish"—but it was absolutely 100-percent true.

Not only was Jack just a guy rather than a god, but I could see him a lot more clearly. Literally. Now it was like I saw through his disguises. Like when I looked closer at him, I saw that his perfectly wolfish grin wasn't nearly so perfect. In addition to his teeth needing a major cleaning, his front tooth was a little chipped.

"What's the matter?" he asked.

Had his voice always been so nasal? Had I just not noticed until that moment?

"Nothing," I replied. That wasn't a lie. Nothing *was* the matter. In fact, it was all good.

He scooted closer to me. "You sure?" he asked, suspiciously.

I nodded absentmindedly, but didn't say anything. Somehow, I didn't think "I've realized that you're just a regular old human being and not a reincarnation of Dante or the guy I want to spend my next five lifetimes with" was a very polite thing to say.

"You positive?"

"Yeah. Why?"

As he put his arm around me, I sniffed. Was that soup? Had he always smelled like soup? How could I have missed the soup smell? "I dunno. You just seem . . . different. You're not mad at me, are you?" he asked anxiously.

"No, Jack. I'm not mad at you," I sighed. There it was again. He never cared about me, or anyone really. He just cared about what people thought about *him*. And the fact that I thought he was a thief? To be a criminal, he would have actually had to think about things other than himself, like getaway cars and where to buy black ski masks.

"I don't know what it is, but girls are always getting mad at me," he went on. He shook his head and sighed. "It's like I just can't win. You say something nice in the moment, and then before you know it they're trying to cash the check at the bank and they get all mad at you when it bounces." He raked his hand through his hair. "How am I supposed to know how I'm going to feel three weeks from now?" He shook his head. "Here we are, living in a society that's always telling us to live in the moment, but when someone then actually *does* that?" He snorted. "Man, it's like a federal offense." He turned to me. "What do you think, Red?"

"What do I think about what?"

"About why all these girls insist on thinking that if I say 'I love you' at some point, it actually . . . *means* something."

I looked over at him, flabbergasted. But he had caught a glance of his face in the side mirror and was too busy checking out his profile to see how my jaw dropped so far you could've fit an entire motorcycle in my mouth. "Because, Jack, it *does* mean something," I retorted. "In fact, it means a lot."

He turned to me, surprised. "Look at you, all feisty!" He gave me one of his smiles that I'd once thought were super-sexy, but that now came off as just plain old creepy. "That's kind of hot."

My response was to scoot closer to the door in case he tried to kiss me. It was funny—not a half hour before I would have killed to hear him call me hot, but now it was just skeezy.

My iPhone buzzed again with another text from Michael.

We're still at Pablo's. Not that you CARE or anything like that, seeing that you've got some wannabe musician as your new BF.

Another text came through.

FYI, just so u know, in case u planned on coming here, Pablo's is at 11482 Hwy 35, in between Hospital Supplies R Us and Applebee's.

Jack snatched the phone away from me and read it. "That's it," he said, turning the ignition and revving the engine as Barbra Streisand filled the air. "We're going to Pablo's so I can kick his butt. No one calls Jack Andrews a 'wannabe musician'!"

I yawned. None of this was exciting anymore. Now it was just exhausting.

twelve

Pablo's Putt-Putt must have been written up in some guidebook for grandparents under "Top Ten Places to Take Your ADD Grandchildren When They Come Visit You in Florida," because when we got there, the place was packed with kids freaking out. I didn't know which was more annoying—having to walk behind old people who moved as slow as snails despite the fact that they were all wearing shiny white Reeboks, or being hit in the head by golf balls shot by screaming eight-year-old boys who couldn't wait until they got to the clown's mouth or dancing cancan girl to tee off.

"So where's your *boyfriend*?" Jack shouted over the blaring salsa music as we made our way through the crowd. I guess it didn't bother any of the old people because none of them could hear anyway.

I rolled my eyes. "I told you—he's not my boyfriend," I yelled, trudging behind him.

He stopped in front of the refreshment stand. "I'll have a chili dog with extra onions, some cheese fries, and a grape Frosty Freez," he said to the guy behind the counter. He turned to me. "I bet your *boyfriend* doesn't eat chili dogs. *Or* onions."

I sighed and ducked as a kid who looked like a pumpkin used his grandfather's cane to whack a golf ball. "I *told* you—I don't *have* a boyfriend anymore. He hit the stop button."

"Yeah, and you wouldn't let me push 'play' again," came a voice from behind me. "What on earth are you wearing on your head?"

I turned around to see Michael standing there in his HIP-HOP HEEB shirt with a girl who—judging from the fact that she definitely had a "booty" and was wearing a pair of leopard-print short-shorts to show it off—had to be Carmen.

Carmen ran her fingers through her dark, curly hair with chunky blonde streaks and looked me up and down. "Wait—*this* is her?" she asked, snapping her gum.

Jack crossed his arms and gave Michael the once-over. Michael crossed *his* arms and glared at him.

Jack turned to me. "You'd rather be with this clown than me?"

"I never said I wanted to be with him! I don't want to be with anyone—I just want to be alone," I said. Sure, the kissing and cuddling part of having a boyfriend was fun, but the other stuff that went along with it? Like, say, the human being part? I wasn't too wild about it. I'd rather date someone I didn't have to actually speak to. Like Dante.

Carmen blew a bubble. "Aw, *chica*, you can't just give up like that! I mean, you might not be eye candy or anything, but that doesn't mean you're gonna end up alone for the rest of your life with cats or something nasty like that. You just gotta practice the power of positive thinking." She walked over and fixed my hat so it wasn't covering my eyes. "You should read that book—whatsitcalled . . . the one that Oprah was goin' off on . . ."

"*The Secret*?" Jack offered.

Carmen turned to him and flashed him a very white smile. "Exactly!" she said with a wink.

"That's twelve bucks, dude," the counter guy said, handing over Jack's food.

"Hey, Red, can you . . . ?" Jack asked, trailing off.

I was so used to paying, I automatically reached for my emergency fund, which had dwindled down to almost nothing. As I was about to hand over the cash, I thought about *Nestled by Need*, when Devon's family held an intervention and sent her to codependency rehab in Arizona after they discovered she was about to harvest her eggs to pay off her Slovakian auto mechanic-slash-sculptor's credit card debt. Would that be me in five years? No food to eat, my clothes hanging off my body—because I had given all my emergency fund money to yet

224

another guy. Would I be standing in front of a circle of people saying, "Hi, my name is Sophie, and I'm addicted to kinda-hot guys who ride motorcycles and are way into themselves"?

Just before Jack could grab the bills, I snatched my hand back. "Actually . . . no, sorry—I can't," I said, shoving the money in my pocket. "This money is supposed to be for emergencies, and last time I checked, a chili dog wasn't an emergency." The minute the words left my mouth I felt like I grew two inches and my boobs grew a cup size. For the first time in forever, I was standing up straight and not slumping.

"But I have hunger pains," he whined. "I'd call that an emergency."

"Well, I don't," I said, "and it's *my* emergency fund." Even my voice sounded different—deeper, like it was coming from my belly and not my head.

Carmen reached into the pocket of her short-shorts and took out her own money. "*Chica,* I get the grrl power thing, but you can't let your man *starve* to death," she said as she handed it over to the counter guy.

"He's not my man," I said in my new strong voice.

Michael let out a sigh of relief. "Oh, thank God. You're back to normal! I have to say, I was a little worried there, Sophie. I mean, I don't want to be dating a crazy girl. Maybe it was being out in the sun that did it. You know you really should wear sunblock." He reached over and tried to take my hat off. "Or maybe it's the hat. Didn't I tell you you're not a red cowboy hat kind of girl?"

I pushed his hands away from me. "But *you're* not my man either, Michael."

Carmen stopped the semi-X-rated version of fry-eating she was doing for Jack's benefit. "Oh, honey, what are you talking about? A girl *needs* a guy, *chica*." She motioned to Michael. "Even if, you know, it's someone like him."

Did a girl need a guy? Jordan had once told me there was this famous saying: *A woman needs a man like a fish needs a bicycle.* I wasn't sure if that was true, but my legs sure were tired from pedaling—especially since it felt like it had all been uphill.

"Nope, I'm done," I announced. "The whole guy thing is way too much trouble."

Jack took a big bite of his chili dog and shook his head. "My shrink would say that's just your fear of intimacy talking, Red," he said with his mouth full. "You can't *not* make a decision—you have to pick one of us." He walked over to the box of putters and took out two of them. "I have a great idea—we'll decide for you. Nine holes, no do-overs. Whoever wins not only gets the free soda, but gets you," he said, throwing a putter toward Michael, who missed it completely.

I couldn't believe this. "What happened to the whole stray-dog/girlfriend's-such-an-ugly-word thing?" I asked.

He shrugged. "Maybe I finally realized what a catch

226

you are, Red. But regardless, it's not like I'm gonna let this clown beat me at something."

Of course he wasn't. Clearly, no one was listening to me when I said I was done with guys and wanted to be alone. "So you're going to play *putt-putt* to decide who gets to be with me?!" I asked. When men fought for Devon's heart it was with yacht races or polo games in sexy, exotic locales—not a miniature golf course in humid, buggy Florida, surrounded by screaming kids and old people.

Carmen, who was now sitting on a motorized plastic horse filing her nails, looked up. "Hey, *chica*, I know you say you wanna be alone, but I can tell you from personal experience, I've been there and it's not fun," she said, cracking her gum. "I was in between boyfriends for five whole days once and it was just horrible." She motioned me over. "If you want a different class of guy, you need to rethink your look." She pointed to my red and white polka-dotted dress. "It's kind of, I don't know, what a character in one of those fairy-tale stories would wear. I am, however, loving the motorcycle boots. If you want, I'll take you to the mall, and we can use that emergency fund of yours to pick out some new stuff." She pointed to her shorts. "They had these in a zebra print too. You have slamming legs. I bet you'd look jalapeño hot in them."

"Yeah, thanks. The thing is, I spent all my money on food for him," I said, pointing at Jack.

* * * * *

227

By the third hole, the two of them were bickering so much about the stupidest things ("You're not allowed to switch clubs midway through the game!" Jack yelled; "Says who? The putt-putt police?!" Michael yelled back) that I was wondering whether I should hang out with Jordan's friend Isis and see if I had any lesbian tendencies and could possibly switch to girls.

I watched as Jack popped out from behind the volcano at the sixth hole each time Michael was about to take a swing, trying to scare him. Why was I sitting here again? "They're acting more immature than those eight-year-olds over there," I said to Carmen, who was sitting with me in the sandy moat surrounding the castle and painting her nails Dark as Midnight.

She shrugged. "I read that guys don't reach the same maturity level as girls until they're *thirty*."

Maybe I didn't need to become a lesbian. Maybe I just needed to date a much older guy. Like *thirty*. Something told me my parents wouldn't go for that, though.

Carmen blew on her nails and pointed at mine. "Want me to do yours? Girl, that blue is *nasty*. I have some remover in my bag."

"Sure." It wasn't like I had anything better to do.

As she painted my nails, Jack stomped over from the clown's head at the seventh hole and, after unchaining his wallet, jammed it in my purse. "The weight of this is completely screwing up my swing. Guard it with your life, okay, Red?" he said, stomping back.

I don't know why he was so worried—it wasn't like there was any *money* in it.

"The two of them fighting over you like this? It's just so *romantic*," Carmen said as she painted away. "Like something out of a book." I could tell that when she was a kid, she probably never stayed within the lines when coloring, because she was getting an awful lot of polish on my fingers.

Carmen was right—it was like a book. But unlike the books I liked to read, it wasn't romantic or fun. It was just . . . exhausting. "Maybe it's not supposed to be so exciting," I said.

"It's not?" Carmen said, confused.

"No, it's not. Maybe my grandmother's right, and life's supposed to be boring most of the time," I said, starting to pace and smearing my wet nails on my dress in the process. "So in those moments where there is something truly exciting, you'll know, and appreciate it that much more." I stopped pacing and looked at Carmen. "Plus, the truth is, this whole . . . *thing* isn't even about me. The guys may say it is, but it's really just all about them and their dumb egos."

"Yeah, well, good luck finding a guy where it's not about his ego," she replied. She pointed to my nails again. "You want me to fix those?"

I looked down at my hands smeared with Dark as Midnight. Who was I kidding? They looked horrible. Even if they had been painted correctly rather than looking like

I had dipped my fingers in the bottle, me plus Dark as Midnight equaled . . . *wrong*. With my pale skin, it made me look like I belonged in a morgue. Maybe Lulu and Carmen could pull it off, but I was still always going to look best in pale pink. It may have been boring, but now that I had come to the realization that life in general wasn't supposed to be a constant emotional roller-coaster ride, it didn't really matter. Why try and fight who I really was?

She took out a bottle of bright, sparkly purple. "We could do this one instead."

"Um, thanks, but I think I'll just go without it for the time being," I replied. "Let them just breathe." When I reached inside my purse for a tissue, Jack's wallet fell out. As I was putting it back in, it flipped open and I saw a folded-up hundred dollar bill. Okay, maybe it didn't exactly flip open by itself—maybe it was more like I opened it— but still, I saw the bill.

Jack hadn't had any money before—just mine. Where had this come from? He couldn't actually be a thief, could he?

I looked over to where Michael was about to hit the ball between the hip-swaying hula dancer's legs, his brows all mushed together like Ali's shar-pei because he was concentrating so hard. I knew he wasn't my boyfriend anymore, and it wasn't like I wanted him back or anything— especially when I saw his belly shake like Jell-O when he wiped his sweaty face with the bottom of his T-shirt—but I couldn't help but worry about his safety.

"What's wrong, *chica*?" asked Carmen. "You're all pale."

I stood up. "I . . . think the butter on the popcorn might have been bad. I'll be right back."

Weaving my way between the little kids and their grandparents, almost crashing into an old man on a motorized scooter, I made my way to the bathroom. Once I locked myself in a stall, I whipped out my iPhone to call Lulu. If anyone would know how to handle this, it was her. But as I went to push the button, I stopped myself. Who was I kidding? Lulu was *nuts*. And I had watched enough detective shows to figure out what to do myself.

I could call the cops. But if I called the police, and Jack was arrested, and there was a trial and he was found guilty, what would I do if he put a hit out on my family from jail? And how would I keep Jack busy until they arrived? This was harder than I thought.

Michael. I had to tell Michael what was going on.

I found the guys at the last hole, and I knew that the planets had gone totally haywire.

Jack and Michael had stopped fighting over me, and were now total BFFs.

Mercury or whatever was *definitely* in retrograde.

"Red, you didn't tell me that Michael was going to be an intern at a record company this summer!" Jack boomed. "That's even cooler than my buddy who won that radio contest where he got to spend a week as a roadie on the

Gods of Metal tour." He turned to Michael and punched him in the arm. "Dude, you da bomb!"

Michael flinched and rubbed his arm. "Thanks, bro," he said. He turned to me. "I told Jack that I want to try and hook him up with Dogz Howz so they can do a duet. Kind of a Kid Rock–redneck-meets-inner-city thing."

"Man, I *love* that idea—it's so five minutes in the future," Jack said. "But I prefer 'nouveau classic rock' rather than 'redneck.'"

"That's cool," Michael said.

I turned to see what Carmen thought of all this, but she was nowhere to be found. "Where's Carmen?"

"She got bored and went to Pizza Hut with some guys from a gospel group," Jack said. "Hey, can I have my wallet back?"

I froze. If I said no, he'd know something was up. But the police would probably be really grateful that I was saving them time by presenting them with the evidence.

"You still have it, right?" he asked.

I reached into my bag and took it out. "Yup. Right here."

He reached out his hand to take it from me.

"But I don't mind holding on to it," I said, not letting go of the wallet.

He yanked at it. "No, it's okay. It's my wallet, and I should carry it. Especially since, you know, you want to be *alone*."

232

"It's okay. Really," I insisted, yanking back.

He gave me a weird look and tugged so hard not only did I let go, but I almost fell in the process. "I don't want to get all in your business, Red, but you might want to look at that codependency stuff."

I grabbed Michael by the arm and started marching him to the corner. "Will do. Can you excuse us for a second?" I yelled over my shoulder.

"*Ow*," Michael said, rubbing his arm. "What's your *problemo*?"

"My *problemo* is that your new BFF is a criminal," I whispered.

We looked over at Jack, now talking to a girl with pink hair and a nose ring who was examining his snake tattoo.

Michael rolled his eyes. "Give me a break. Is that what happened to that chick Devon in one of your books?"

"Yes, as a matter of fact, it kind of did," I replied. It happened in *Smitten by Surprise*, when Devon returned to L.A. after being in New York for Fashion Week to find that not only had her old lover and her new lover become friends, but they had actually fallen in love with each other before her old lover found out that her new lover was a criminal. "But I don't have time to sit here so you can make fun of me when we're in danger."

I filled him in on the details about the break-in, the hundred dollars, everything.

"Okay, maybe it *does* sound a little strange," Michael conceded when I was done. "But I'm sure there's a rational explanation for all of it. He seems like a really good guy. Maybe . . . I don't know . . . the hundred-dollar bill is like, I don't know, emergency money from his mom or something."

"If it's emergency money, then why have *I* been paying for everything?"

"You have? You never pay for me."

I rolled my eyes. When I got back to school, I was going to have to ask Mr. Dreyer, the biology teacher, if there was something in male DNA that made them all self-centered.

He shrugged. "I don't know what to tell you. I really think you're overreacting. I'm gonna go finish our game now. We're on the last hole."

He was no help. "By the way—who's winning?" I asked, curiosity getting the best of me.

"I'm not sure. We stopped keeping score a while ago."

"But . . ."

"But what?"

"How are you going to know who gets to date me?" I asked.

"You said you didn't want to date either of us anyway," he said.

True, but it had been the point of the whole putt-putt game!

"We'll figure that part out later," he said as he continued walking.

Maybe my life wasn't like a romance novel after all. Because in a romance novel, the two guys who were fighting for the girl would actually *fight* for the girl rather than trust it would all just figure itself out.

thirteen

After what seemed like an eternity (even though it was only ten minutes), the guys finished the last hole and it was finally time to leave. With Carmen gone, Jack and I were stuck having to drive Michael back. Not that I minded. Having Michael there made me feel safer. Plus, the idea of being alone with Jack and having to listen to him talk about himself some more wasn't very appealing. Of course, now that he and Jack were best friends, it wasn't like Michael was any better. Not to mention the fact that if worse came to worst, Michael would have no clue what to do in case of an emergency.

Like, for instance, if we got a flat tire on the highway.

"Don't you just want to call Triple A and wait for them?" Michael said nervously after we had pulled over to the shoulder.

Jack shook his head. "Triple A's for amateurs," he scoffed.

As he opened the driver's side door, the loud rumble of eighteen-wheeler trucks filled the air. It was already eleven at night, and the highway was deserted except for them. It was definitely creepy—like something out of a horror movie about killer trucks.

"You know, when I was in the car with my dad recently, there was a story on the radio about how truck drivers take uppers so they can drive all night and that it's almost as bad as if they were drunk driving," Michael said.

"Yeah?" Jack said.

"So what if we're changing the tire and one of them crashes into us!"

Jack's eyes narrowed. "You've never changed a tire before, have you?" Even I knew how to do that, thanks to that Driver's Ed/defensive driving course I took last fall.

"I have so," Michael said defensively.

From the backseat, I stopped trying to call Grandma Roz and looked up. "What, on your Big Wheel when you were five?"

He turned and gave me a dirty look. "It wasn't my Big Wheel. It was my Tiny Trike."

Jack reached across Michael and opened the passenger door as well. "It's about time you became a man. Believe me, you'll thank me for this one day."

"Why will I thank you after ending up with grease on my shirt?" Michael asked.

After they got out of the car, I locked the doors and

went back to calling my grandmother so I could let her know about the flat. Oddly, the phone just rang and rang. Even if she was sleeping, she should have heard it, because she always slept with the phone right next to her ear in case someone called in the middle of the night with news that someone had died.

I heard the guys rummaging around in the trunk, then a loud thump followed by Jack screaming, "My foot! My foot!"

"It's not like I did it on *purpose*," I heard Michael say.

There was more thumping, and when I looked up I saw Jack hopping back to the car while Michael trailed behind. "Who has a bowling ball in their trunk but no jack?" I heard him say.

"You need to elevate that," I said, pinching my nose as I examined Jack's foot. A foot that had been in a motorcycle boot all day smelled really gross, especially when it was in a car with the windows closed.

"I do?"

"Yeah. Or else it'll swell."

"Wow, Red—you *are* really smart."

I shrugged. "Girl Scouts."

We went with Michael's original plan of calling AAA ("Too bad no one bothered to listen to me in the first place," he grumbled), then settled in and waited for them to arrive. When they wouldn't stop fighting about what radio station to listen to, I made Michael switch seats with me and

I took control—landing on a talk show where a guy talked about how he had been abducted by aliens a few months before and how, ever since then, he could see people's inner thoughts in a cartoon bubble above their heads.

Unfortunately, none of us remembered that listening to the radio when you have the engine off drains the battery. Which meant that even after Luther, the AAA guy, changed the tire, we couldn't go anywhere because the battery was dead. And the Buick was so old, it wouldn't take a jump start. Which meant that the three of us had to pile into the front seat of Luther's truck and have the Buick towed.

Smooshed in between my two ex-soul mates—one with a smelly foot and another with a rumbling stomach thanks to all the junk food he ate—I thought about fate. What if I had gone to Mexico with Jordan? Would I have met a *different* soul mate? Someone whose eyes I would have been staring into this very minute as the tropical breezes gave my hair a cool windblown look and we ate guacamole? Or was my fate that my Spring Break was *supposed* to have been exactly like this—in humid Florida, with frizzy hair, learning the painful lesson that there *wasn't* such a thing as a soul mate. That no matter how good someone's butt looked in faded jeans, or how good their fashion sense, they were just human, with smelly feet and gassy stomachs, and all that other icky stuff that wasn't romantic but was part of real life.

Was my fate that I was supposed to learn that guys like Dante didn't exist in real life? That he was just a character who had been made up so that people could escape reality every once in a while? And that the hot guys who rode motorcycles were overrated and not much better than the ones who used hand sanitizer all the time?

I turned to Jack, who had fallen asleep with his head against the back of the seat and was snoring quietly. Then I turned to Michael, who was also sleeping, with his head against the window, and also snoring quietly.

Then I turned to Luther, who was softly singing along to some cheesy love song about how some guy was going to love this girl until the end of time, before he took his index finger and started rooting around in his right nostril.

Yup. At the end of the day, humans were all just really . . . *human.*

"Luther?" I whispered.

He quickly took his finger out of his nose and turned to me. "Yeah?"

"Are you married?"

He nodded and held up his left hand where I could see a big gold ring. "Thirty-nine years," he sighed.

"Is it hard?"

"Hard?! Sometimes I wake up and turn to her and I think, 'Man, *you* again?'"

"So she annoys you sometimes?"

"Sometimes?! Try most of the time."

I could feel my stomach start to clench. Love wasn't supposed to be a jail sentence, was it?

"But I wouldn't trade a minute of it," he went on. "I love her just as much as the day we met."

My stomach unclenched. "You do?"

He nodded. "Yup. I'm not sayin' I believe in soul mates or any of that junk, but if I'm gonna spend my life bein' with just one person, I'm sure glad it's her."

Maybe *that's* why I was supposed to come to Florida—to hear Luther say that.

Or maybe I was supposed to come to Florida to find out that nothing was what it seemed—not supposedly hot bad boys who may or may not have been criminals, not perfect boyfriends, and *especially* not arthritic old men who jingled their pocket change.

We pulled up to Grandma Roz's condo, and I saw three police cars with flashing lights out front. My heart started to race. All these years I had joked that Grandma Roz was a hypochondriac—but what if something had finally happened to her? As we got closer to the condo, however, I saw her standing outside wiggling her finger in front of a policeman's face, and I breathed a sigh of relief. She was fine.

As the three of us got out of the truck, I realized this might be my last time with Jack where we weren't separated by a bulletproof partition of glass. I put my hand on his arm and turned to Michael. "Do you think Jack and I can have a moment?"

He yawned and nodded, shuffling off to sit on the curb and eat his taco from Taco Bell. I guess whatever jealousy he had been feeling had officially sizzled out after he had convinced Luther to go through the drive-through on the way back.

"What's up, Red?" Jack asked, also yawning. Obviously, he hadn't seen the cops and had no idea that life as he had known it was officially over. I wondered if they had Pizza Fridays in jail like they did in middle school.

I tipped my hat up so I could get one last look at his face and, like Devon had done with Dante, "memorize every last curve and crevice of his rugged countenance" (and, in Jack's case, the big red zit on his forehead that had popped up during the drive back from Pablo's). Maybe he was a super-self-involved human, with oil glands and everything, but he'd always hold the space in my heart marked "First Big Dramatic Adventure." My hat was so big, it kept flopping down and ruining the moment, so I finally just took it off. "I just wanted to say," I began, "no matter what happens when we walk in that door . . ." I grabbed his hand and tried not to cringe at how sticky it was from all the junk food he had eaten. "I don't regret a single moment we've had together."

"So you really are breaking up with me, huh?" he asked.

I nodded. Even if I had wanted to be with Jack, I didn't think I could do the long-distance/convict thing.

"Wow. No one's ever broken up with me. Either *I* break up with *them*, or I just end up splitting without an explanation."

Suddenly, Grandma Roz came barreling toward us. "Ach! Thank God you're here!" she bellowed, pulling Jack and I into a bear hug and smothering us between her boobs. I didn't know what was freaking me out more: that she was hugging a criminal, or that she was wearing a fuchsia silk nightgown with black lace that was so low-cut her boobs were almost falling out.

"You have no idea what I've been through these last few hours. I'm surprised I haven't dropped dead from a heart attack," she said once she let us go.

Just then two cops walked out, one on either side of Art, who was in handcuffs.

"What's going on?" I asked.

"That . . . *animal*," she replied, pointing at him, "was the one who broke into the condo."

"No he's not," I blurted out. I pointed at Jack. "*He's* the one who broke into the condo."

"Huh?" Jack said, confused.

I reached for his wallet and opened it, yanking out the hundred-dollar bill. "See? This is the only thing he managed to get before we walked in and caught him."

"That's not mine," Grandma Roz said. "I keep all my

cash underneath my mattress, and when I went to check this afternoon, all 75,562 dollars and 33 cents was there."

Jack looked so upset, you'd think I had accused him of murder. "That's the hundred-dollar in-case-of-emergency bill my grandmother gave me," he said.

"I told you!" Michael said from the curb.

"But . . . but . . . but the whole trip you made me pay for everything. You said you didn't have any money!" I exclaimed.

Jack shrugged. "Well, lunch at Denny's doesn't exactly qualify as an emergency."

Jack wasn't a criminal—he was just cheap. I should have known.

"It's a good thing you broke up with me, Red," he sighed dramatically. "'Cause I don't think I could be with some-one who would think I could ever do something as horrible as steal from a senior citizen." He flashed Grandma Roz his trademark grin. "Especially someone as wonderful as your grandma."

I rolled my eyes. Not only was he cheap; he was a suck-up to boot.

"You can't put a man in jail without his hearing aid!" Art was screaming as the cops dragged him toward the squad car. When they got to Grandma Roz, he stopped.

"This doesn't mean you're going to stop loving me now, *bubelah*, does it?" he asked anxiously.

She paused and thought about it for a second. "I don't

know, Art. I'm going to have to really search my soul about that one."

He shrugged. "Okay. Just let me know when you decide," he said as the police pulled him along to the car.

After Grandma Roz changed into a more respectably grandmotherly velour tracksuit, the four of us hitched a ride in one of the cop cars to the precinct. After an hour, a detective came out of the interrogation room and filled us in. It turned out that over the last few years, not only had Art stolen thousands of dollars in bonds from Grandma Roz, but when he wasn't shuttling her around to early bird special dinners or senior citizen-priced matinees, he was with his *other* lady friends—stealing from them!

"*Oy gevalt!*" Grandma Roz cried. "The money I may have been able to forgive—but he had other lady friends?! What—I wasn't enough for him?"

"Huh. So *that's* why he kept asking if I knew where he could get a fake ID," Jack said. "And that explains why I found him online on Craigslist checking apartment listings in Buenos Aires."

"He was?" I asked. Jack and I had hardly spent a moment apart for days, but I hadn't seen any of that. Here I was, upset that Jack and Michael were all about themselves and their dramas, and I was so wrapped up in my own world that I had totally missed *this* drama. Which was pretty juicy.

While the detective helped Grandma Roz fill out a mountain of paperwork, Jack went to go flirt with the cleaning lady and Michael and I started up a game of Go Fish. I was winning when Jack ambled up to me.

"Hey, Red, can I talk to you a sec?"

"Okay," I shrugged.

We walked over to the corner. "I've been thinking about it, and I think us breaking up is the right way to go."

Um, great. Hadn't I already said that?

"The truth is you deserve a lot better than me." He sighed and shook his head. "I don't know—it must be that stray dog thing. Sometimes I wonder if I'll ever be able to settle down."

He looked so vulnerable just then. Some of those old feelings almost came flooding back, but I willed myself to stay strong.

"I guess when I finally meet the perfect person, it won't be an issue," he went on. "When I meet her, I'll be so happy I could be locked in a *doghouse* and be happy about it if she's with me!" He hugged me. "Thanks, Red."

"For what?"

"For helping me get more clear on what I want in a girl." He gave me one of those sweet smiles that, up until that afternoon, had made my blood-sugar level shoot up. "You're really great, you know that?"

I had helped him decide what he didn't want. Talk about a backhanded compliment. I unstuck my hand from his and sighed. I knew I had made the right decision.

I debated going off and enlightening him about everything I had realized in the last few hours—about his self-obsession; about how perfect people only existed in books and movies; and that, like Luther said, relationships were work. Maybe it wasn't super-exciting every moment, but the feeling of knowing someone so well that you could finish their sentences for them was actually pretty cool. Almost like you became psychic or something.

Then I realized that if I had to go through the pain of learning all that firsthand, Jack should too. It'd be good for him.

"Thanks, Jack. That's really sweet," I replied.

He nodded. "Well, I think I'm gonna get going now." He motioned to the cleaning girl who had finished up and was putting her coat on. "Lori says there's a Denny's not too far from here, so we're gonna go get something to eat. I hope she's got some cash on her." He hugged me. "Thanks for everything, Red. It's been really fun hanging with you."

I hugged him back. That soup smell had gotten stronger. "Good-bye, Jack."

"Hey, you didn't happen to get that Carmen girl's number by any chance, did you?" he asked.

"No. Sorry," I said.

"Oh well. Probably better that way. I'm trying not to do the long-distance relationship thing anymore anyway. Those things can drag on forever."

As he walked toward Lori, he turned back around and pointed at my boots. "I'm glad I got you those, Red. Even though things didn't work out with us, I hope you'll still wear them. And that when you do, you'll think of me."

I nodded. I would. As much as I thought I was over him, I could still feel my eyes fill up. Jack may have been a cheap, self-involved suck-up, but he did have a sensitive side.

I headed back toward Michael, who, along with about five cops, was engrossed in an Animal Planet documentary that was blaring from the TV mounted on the wall.

"You don't have to stay, you know. Grandma Roz and I can get back on our own," I told him.

He shrugged. "It's okay," he said, not looking away from the TV.

"Yeah, but it's three o'clock in the morning."

He shrugged again. "It's only midnight L.A. time."

"Yeah, but you've been sick," I said. "Why don't you just call a cab and go back to your grandmother's?"

He turned to me. "Why do you always have to 'yeah, but' me?" he snapped. "Police stations can be dangerous, and unlike *some* people, I'd never just take off and leave you surrounded by criminals."

I looked around. Other than a man wearing tight jeans and a hot-pink polo shirt, who was demanding that someone do a sketch of his lost Chihuahua, and a few cops (including a policewoman who I saw was reading Lulu's book *Flushed with Fantasy*), there was no one else in the place. I opened my mouth to say, "Yeah, but . . ." and stopped myself.

"Okay, maybe there aren't any here at this very moment, but you never know," he said. "A bunch of them could come in any second."

"Yeah, but—"

He rolled his eyes.

"—you're not my boyfriend anymore," I said softly. "You don't have to do this kind of stuff."

"Sophie, did you ever think maybe I *want* to do it?"

That hadn't occurred to me. I thought about it. "No."

"Well, maybe I do." He turned to me. "I . . . I want to be here for you, okay?"

"You do?"

He gave one of his overly loud, overly drawn-out sighs that he saved for when he was *really* annoyed with me. "Yes. I do."

"Oh." I said softly. I was surprised to feel the tingling in the bottom of my spine that I had felt when I saw him walking over to me the day we met at Faryl's Bat Mitzvah.

"Is that okay?" he asked.

I felt my face get hot. "Sure. I guess so," I said shyly.

"Okay then," he said. "But will you do me a favor?"

"What?"

He pointed to my hat. "Do you think you can take that thing off? It's—"

"It's what? Stupid? Silly-looking?" I demanded angrily. "No, Michael, I can't take it off. It completely symbolizes my innermost self, and if you can't accept that"—I pushed the hat up so I could actually see him—"then I guess there's nothing to talk about."

"All I was going to say was that it's hard to see your eyes when you have it on, 'cause it's too big for you," he replied. "And you have such great eyes, I thought you'd want people to see them."

My eyes narrowed. He had never said anything like that before. Had being around Jack rubbed off on him? Was he trying out some line? "What color are they?" I said suspiciously.

"They're green. The same shade as the Notre Dame Fighting Irish green."

Huh. I had no idea Michael could be so poetic.

He lifted the hat off my head. "You know what? I know I said you weren't a red cowboy hat kind of girl back at the Dell, but it's sort of growing on me."

"It is?"

"Yeah, but it's way too big. If you want, when we get back to L.A., I'll go with you to that western store on Sunset Boulevard so you can get one that actually fits."

"You will?"

He nodded. "Sure." He pointed at my feet. "Oh, and I'm digging the boots. I never would have thought they'd work, but they're very you."

"Thanks," I said with a smile. I stood up. I had an idea. "I'll be right back," I said. I walked over to the policewoman. "Excuse me—would you like this?" I asked, holding the hat out to her.

She looked up and gasped. "Oh my. That hat—it's just like—"

I pointed at the book. "—the one Devon's wearing in the book. Minus the feathers." I shoved it toward her. "Try it on."

She took it from me and placed it on her rather large head.

"It fits perfectly. You sure you don't want it anymore?" she asked. She reached up and squeezed it. "This is grade-A felt."

"I know, but it's time for me to find one that's a better fit," I replied, turning to make my way back to Michael.

epilogue

The first thing I did when I got back to L.A. was take all my Devon books, box them up, and put them in the garage. I'd already read them all, and after everything I had been through, it didn't feel like I needed them anymore. As I set the box down, I was tempted to start reading some of the other books Mom had stored out there—especially one called *Hollywood Wives* by Jackie Collins, because when I flipped through, it seemed to have *a lot* of really juicy scenes. But the more I thought about it, the more I realized I should be living my life for a while, rather than reading about someone else's. In fact, instead of "WWDDD?" I decided to make my new motto "WWSGD?"—*What would Sophie Greene do?* Sure, it might take a little longer to come up with an answer, since there was a big difference between what a sixteen-year-old girl would do and what a thirtysomething, jet-setting, fling-having, jewelry-designing woman would do, but I knew it would be worth the effort.

And when it came to Michael Rosenberg, it turned out that what Sophie Greene would do was give him another chance. It wasn't like Florida had turned him into a brand-new person—he still paid more attention to the TV than to me when we were on the phone—but he *was* more affectionate. He even came up with a nickname for me, Motorcycle Mama, because of the boots that I continued to wear all the time (after Mom took one look at them and sent them to the shoemaker to have them disinfected).

But when, a few weeks later, word spread through the cafeteria that Juliet DeStefano was moving again (the rumors covered everything from pregnancy to getting offered a job as Angelina Jolie's stand-in—but because we were now friends, I knew it was because her dad was being transferred) and Michelle Goldman told me that they had to rework the calendar and that Miss April was mine if I wanted it, I knew that Devon and I would both say the same thing—yes.

By then, I was officially off drama for forty-five days (no Devon, no SOAPnet—cold turkey), so I was crystal clear that drama was overrated. And I knew that being Miss April wasn't going to drastically change my life or anything. But still, you never knew—it might change it a *teensy* bit. Like by, say, pushing me over the edge with the admissions committees who reviewed my college applications.

When the day of the photo shoot came, I decided to still wear the milkmaid dress, but I ditched the cute little cardigan and added my new red cowboy hat—the one that Michael and I picked out, which actually fit—and my motorcycle boots.

When Michael saw the pictures, he said I looked phat. Which, according to UrbanDictionary.com means "pretty hot and tempting."

And that's exactly what the Nigerian prince-slash-cabdriver called Devon in *Infatuated by Intrigue*.

Turn the page for an excerpt of *Cindy Ella*!

978-0-14-240392-1

Prom fever has infected L.A.—especially Cindy's two annoying stepsisters and her overly Botoxed stepmother. Cindy seems to be the only one immune to it all. Once Cindy's anti-prom letter is published in the school newspaper, everyone thinks she's committed social suicide—everyone except her two best friends and, shockingly, the most popular senior at Castle Heights High and Cindy's crush, Adam Silver. But, with a little help from an unexpected source—and the perfect pair of shoes—Cindy realizes that she still has a chance at a happily-ever-after.

prologue

It was the Thursday after Memorial Day and the entire day had been a walking nightmare: snickers, whispers, conversations that ground to a halt whenever I entered the room. The kind of stuff that really pumps up a fifteen-and-a-half-year-old girl's self-esteem. As you can imagine, with the name Cindy Ella Gold, I was used to a fair amount of teasing, but nothing like what I experienced that day.

There I was thinking I was being of service to my fellow nonpopular/nonpromgoing classmates by being the official "We're Not Going to Take It" poster girl, but instead of gratitude and respect, all I got were dirty looks and a schoolwide silent treatment. Even the weirdest kids in school—like Eliza Nesbit, who wore reindeer sweaters all winter, and Maury Scheinberg, who spoke in video-game-speak instead of English—wouldn't look me in the eye. Within the course of a few hours, I had gone from being just another average kid to the most untouchable Untouchable of Castle Heights High.

1

"Why'd *this* have to be the letter they finally printed?" I moaned to my two BFFs, India and Malcolm, as we sat under our bougainvillea tree that day eating our lunches. The smell of clove cigarettes wafted over from a group of girls dressed in black who were taking turns reading their Sylvia Plath–lite journal entries aloud. "Why couldn't they have printed the one about how the cafeteria should be demolished so no one has to go through the awful experience of figuring out where to sit?"

"You don't think you'll have to be homeschooled now, do you?" asked Malcolm.

I ignored him. He could be such a drama queen at times. "I mean, I knew what I wrote would piss the popular kids off," I said as I took a bite of my sandwich and watched a big glop of tuna fall onto my brand-new CULTURAL ICON IN TRAINING T-shirt. "But I honestly thought everyone else would be thrilled that someone was finally taking a stand about how the prom is just one more attempt by the establishment to keep us down."

"What are you talking about?" Malcolm stopped his lunchtime ritual of inspecting his khakis for the tiniest speck of dirt and looked up, sighing as his eyes zeroed in on my latest attempt to accessorize with tuna.

"You know, how the prom separates the haves from the have-nots; the popular from the unpopular—" I stopped, as Malcolm started frantically rubbing at the blossoming stain on my nonexistent boobs.

2

"Those who take deep full breaths from their core instead of quick shallow ones," finished India, whose parents owned a chain of yoga studios in town called Blissed Out. "Cin, you spoke the truth—but unfortunately it's one of those dirty little truths that people don't like to think about. They'd rather remain ignorant than search within for answers." She stood up and stretched before settling into a down-dog pose. "A tree doesn't grow branches with water alone, right?" she said. With her long blond hair covering her face, she looked like a supergorgeous version of Cousin It from *The Addams Family*.

Malcolm and I looked at each other, baffled. "Huh?" we said. Even though I've known India for years, and even worked part-time at one of the studios on Sundays, and was therefore used to hearing this kind of Zen mumbo jumbo on a regular basis, it still tended to go over my head.

"Never mind." India sighed from behind her hair.

"Look, what it comes down to is that no one who's unpopular wants to be reminded of that," said Malcolm. "They want to believe that if they just hold on long enough, they, too, can pull a Farmer Ted." Farmer Ted was the character that Anthony Michael Hall played in *Sixteen Candles* who went from geekness to greatness in ninety-one minutes. Malcolm processed everything in life by comparing it to eighties movies. Ms. Highland, our guidance counselor, was convinced it was some sort of personality disorder.

India rejoined us on the ground. "Hey, Wally, I'm so

with you in spirit!" she yelled out to Wally Twersky, Castle Heights's resident tree hugger, as he strummed "We Shall Overcome" on his guitar for the tenth straight lunch period as part of his protest against the fact that the school had uprooted endangered trees from across the country and replanted them here in an attempt to spruce up the campus grounds. She patted me on the knee. "I'm sure it'll all blow over by Monday," said India. "Especially after Danny Miller's party this weekend. And *especially* since Jessica Rokosny just got out of rehab."

Malcolm let out a relieved sigh and started inspecting his loafers for scuffs. "Brilliant. With Jessica back, you'll definitely be in the clear." Not only was Jessica a self-taught "pharmacist," she was also the senior-class slut, so the chances of her doing something outrageous to take the focus off of me were pretty good.

"I guess," I said glumly.

"Hey, no matter what happens—you know, if you do end up having to leave school because the teasing gets so bad or what not—you'll always have us," he promised.

Malcolm was right. I *did* have them, and for that I was very grateful. I had met India on the first day of fifth grade when I moved to L.A. from New Jersey, and Malcolm, on our first day at Castle Heights. Malcolm lives in South-Central L.A., so he has to take three buses every day just so he can go to our school, which is supposed to be one of the best in the city, although I have no idea who exactly decides those things. So that they wouldn't be accused of being too elitist, Castle Heights gave out scholarships to underprivileged youth and Malcolm was one of them, even though you'd never be able to tell by looking at his wardrobe and iPod library. But I don't feel sorry for him, because while he may be one of my best friends, he can also be a total diva. He puts La Lohan to shame at times. However, I tend to cut him some slack when he starts to have a meltdown. Finding yourself in a predominantly white private high school after growing up in the 'hood is enough to cause anyone some angst.

The three of us made up what we called the Outsiders' Insider Club. Malcolm's black and gay, so it's pretty obvious why he's an outsider. And India—well, even though we live in L.A., where there's a lot of boho-lite going on, people aren't all that tolerant when it comes to the old-school hippies like India who follow strict hundred percent vegan diets and don't shave their armpits.

And me? In a way I'm even more of an outsider because I'm just normal. I'm not gay and I'm not a hippy. I'm not ugly and I'm not beautiful. I'm thin (more like scrawny), but I have no muscle tone. I'm not remedial-math-class dumb, but I'm not egghead brilliant.

I'm just . . . *average*. At least by L.A. standards. Now, if I lived someplace like Twin Falls, Idaho, maybe I'd be considered kind of special. But here in L.A., where everyone's a size two, looks like an Abercrombie model, and has been on the road to Harvard since preschool? Forget it. At least Malcolm and India are dramatically different. But for me, the normal one who kind of blends into the crowd, growing up in L.A. can be hard. Because here, "normal" equals "invisible."

But that Wednesday I sure wasn't invisible. As I skulked down the hall after lunch, trying to tune out the snickers and whispers that had become the sound track to my life, I prayed that Jessica Rokosny hadn't completely cleaned up her act in rehab. *Are You there, God? It's me, Cindy,* I thought as I wiped off the "Cindy Ella's just pissed 'cuz she's a freak and no one will EVER ask her to prom" graffiti that someone had scrawled on my locker during lunch. *Listen, I'm cool with You keeping Jessica clean and sober,* I thought, *but can You make it so that she ends up making out with at least one inappropriate guy or girl at Danny Miller's party this Saturday so that people will be talking about* that *on Monday and not me?*

I didn't know where I stood on the God thing, and whether I was just wasting my time asking for divine intervention, but I did know that it sucked being a non-prom girl in an all-prom world.

Princess, meet frog . . .

978-0-14-241122-3

Dylan Schoenfield is the princess of L.A.'s posh Castle Heights High. But when she accidentally tosses her bag into a fountain, she comes face-to-face with her own personal frog: self-professed film geek Josh Rosen. Reluctantly, Dylan lets F-list Josh into her A-list world, and is shocked to find herself becoming friends with a geek—and liking it. But when Dylan's so-called prince charming of a boyfriend dumps her flat, her life—and her social status—come to a crashing halt. Can Dylan—with Josh's help—pull the pieces together to create her own happily-ever-after?